THE
WILDERLANDS

R. E. BELLESMITH

This book is a work of fiction. Any resemblance to persons, alive or dead, or real world events contained within the story is coincidental.

Cover art by Sabrina Claman, @cow_turtle_moo on Instagram.

Cover design by Wendy Mach, White Stone Pages.

The Wilderlands

ISBN: 979-8-9905369-7-5

Copyright © 2024, R.E. Bellesmith

For my grandparents

Contents

A THIRD NIGHT

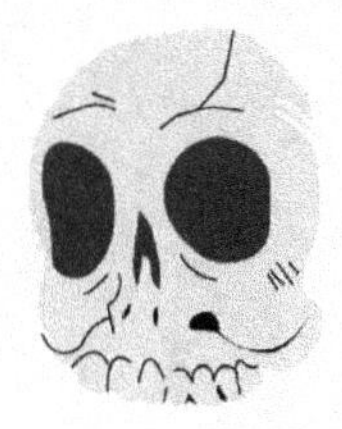

NIGHT
ONE

>>> I <<<

EARS! EARS! ATTEND ME NOW!

Come away from the freezing walls. Gather harthward, hold close those you love, fill your cup. I have an oft told tale from the far west that can spin you away from this warsome winter and the howl-hungry things at our doors. Attend me now, while my bones can still bear it.

Many of the best tellers insist this tale begins with loss, a soul-dragging loss to rattle your ribs. The oldest, and most world-weary will tell you it begins with Death doing the work that befits him. The more eager and less experienced say this story begins with a man, one who swallowed sorrow and loss as much as he dealt it.

In truth, tellers are dishonest folk.

This tale began as all things do: in fire.

It was a single flame-wreathed arrow at first, cutting through the night. Its hundred red wings struggled to keep it in the air—flailing and failing and elegant. As it passed the apex of its journey, a flock of its brethren bit into the night behind it.

For a breath, a beat, a sinful stretch—there was quiet.

Then the fire's wings brushed the top of a wagon, as if flapping to lift the vessel into the air.

Soldiers steamed from the wagons as flames reached out after them. The quick soldiers escaped. The quick and lucky did so unscorched.

Those who were neither were left behind, cooking in their armor, their screams and the shrieks of civilians smothered by the battle-bark of the attackers.

The Wilderfolk were birthed from fear and night. They came like devils, clothed in the skins of wild things and bearing weapons more gnarled and deadly than the most fume-blown beast you ever faced.

Knalc was at the head of this stampede and gave himself to battle as easily as you all hear my words now. His cruel blade split helmet and head from fleeing soldiers; his blackened, bare feet beat past fallen friend and smote foe in same stride. 'Round his neck hung a clay sphere which he protected from dent and damage more than his own human heart.

One soldier—a soul more stupid than brave, more frightened than thoughtful—charged him. "To me!" he screamed to his fellows as he pressed toward Knalc. "To me, men! Protect the wagons! Protect your families!"

Not all tellings of this tale include this death-damned soldier. In those that do, he and Knalc sometimes duel ferociously, leaving naught alive around them. Sometimes the soldier takes a hundred blows, while Knalc endures twice as much. Sometimes Knalc barely even notices the soldier as he shaves head from shoulders in a single swing.

All those accounts agree though, the soldier died there and Knalc persisted, reveling in the flame-wrought ruin of the caravan.

Knalc's lungs stung with ash and smoke and his coywolf pelt grew fat with sopping blood. The nearer he came to the center of the caravan the more soldiers gave way to crying women, whining children, and common men praying to false gods. Knalc's muscles bubbled like wrathful clouds, trailing drops of red rain behind him. He stormed by with the wrath and speed of a summer storm; most knew instinctively to move from his wake—those that didn't screamed and were made silent.

Valforians scrambled from wagons, cradling all manner of the bright and burdensome things the fool-folk from Valian find so precious—even in flame-blistered arms, leaving food and water behind.

Smiling, Knalc slowed his rampage and stepped into the back of one of the covered wagons that had not yet begun to burn. He entered slow-like, steadily breathing the smoke-stained air. He stood still, gorging his eyes on the darkness of the wagon to make them strong against it.

His eyes had not yet had their fill when a knife cut at him.

He moved away without thinking and found his attacker.

A woman.

In the moment he took to laugh, she painted fresh blood across his bare arm. The wound was scarcely more than a scratch, but it killed his laughter.

Knalc warned, awkward-like in Valforian tongue, "Stop."

Howling and crazed, the woman pounced again.

He stepped away, but those Valforian wagons are small, and it only took the woman a moment more to blade-bleed him a second time.

Quick as she came, she shrunk back, admired the wound she had greeted him with, and sprung again to stab his chest.

But Knalc was ready this time. He caught her wrist—the metal weapon pointing the way to his heart.

He remained calm. "Stop."

With another guttural cry, she clawed his face—her fingers raking flesh and drawing blood. Without wanting to, he fell, bringing her with him.

As I tell it to you here, the two of them rolled and shrieked on the floor—like laughing-cats. As I tell it to you here, she didn't beg or cry or coo—but bit and slashed and butted, sinking her teeth so deep into his shoulder she tasted marrow. As she did, she clawed with one hand at his chest, looking to rake the life from his skin but instead brushing the clay heart Knalc had hanging from his neck. As I tell it to you here, he felt her fingers against that cold clay sharper than her teeth in his living flesh. As I tell you all here, he didn't realize he'd slid his blade deep between her ribs until he heard a gut-gurgle and felt her go limp on top of him.

"*Damn*," he hissed in proper-tongue.

He rolled her off. The woman didn't struggle more than a creek-carried branch. She stared up without seeing anything that was there, probably calling on her god to help her. But even gods that ain't false don't oft help the living or the dying.

Like most Valforians, the woman had small hands, the kind that ain't accustomed to holding knives or fighting off coywolves in the night. Those hands were shaking now, grasping at the weeping wound run through her. Blood slipped from between her lips and leaked down her chin. She came back to herself a little at the end and looked at Knalc—in one eye sat Sister Hatred and in the other was Brother Longing. Her mouth moved, failing to form more than brief, bloody bubbles.

Knalc watched, and only moved again when he felt the weight of her life flutter away.

He spat, brushing his hand over the bite on his shoulder. She was Valforian, which meant there was no risk of foam fever. She was young for a Valforian, like as not she had been in her thirties. Valforians made sure to preserve themselves well in life and it's always harder to read their age once Death has done his work.

Knalc snatched up his stabber and cleaned it of the woman's

blood. He started to leave, but something in his innards seized him.

Knowing his guts had always told him true, he turned around to retrieve the woman's knife, tossing out the one already on his belt and replacing it with his new trophy. He didn't even bother to clean his blood from the prize as he stepped from the wagon.

The fighting was beginning to fade. Those who were not lying broken and bloodied had fled into the Wilderlands. As Knalc walked the battlefield, he breathed blood-fumes and burning wood.

"Knalc!"

He turned and found loyal Giemar running toward him through a veil of ash and smoke.

"Knalc," Giemar repeated. *"Come, there's something you won't believe."*

Knalc grunted like a man who believes quite a bit.

Giemar knew that sound. *"You doubt too much. Come!"*

Knalc's vision roved about, searching for the excuse of Valforian soldiers lurking in either soot or shadow who he could kill instead. Those that he found were in Death's lap and would be poor sport, so he sighed and followed Giemar.

Giemar spoke again as they walked. *"What did you find in the wagon?"*

"Same thing we always find," he paused before adding, *"And a woman."*

With a laugh as buxom as a boar's howl, Giemar roared. *"You? A woman? I was beginning to think—"*

"That's not what happened."

"As you say," said Giemar, though he still chuckled in the back of his throat.

"What is it you wanted me to see?"

Giemar nodded ahead, for they had already arrived. *"Look unto it yourself."*

A pack of their tribesmen had gathered 'round one of the overturned wagons, cheering and shouting like they were watching coywolves fight. As Knalc came closer, he saw a Valforian man at the center of this congregation—dressed in a red as dark and gorish as the inside of a man. He brandished a thin blade made of tricksy Valforian steel. At his feet lay the soul-drained shells of two of Knalc's tribesmen.

Knalc was less amused than the congregation. *"What's there to see? Someone kill the bastard and be done with him."*

"Watch," Giemar urged.

Eventually, one of Knalc's tribesmen came forward with enough bravery in his chest to face the man in red. He hefted an ax of healthy size as he prepared to fight. The dirt rumbled to the cheering and chanting of the crowd. We can't know what name they chanted for their tribesman—if he had lived, I would tell you about him rather than Red.

The tribesman began to walk circles 'round the red warrior. His fingers tightening and loosening at his ax handle while the man in red followed him with a keen eye.

The tribesman charged.

Red moved so light-like, Knalc almost didn't see what happened.

The tribesman was two bounds away from him when the Valforian steel snicked him.

The tribesman lost his name then as he fell to the ground, neck spitting blood.

It ain't often you hear of Valforians being honored by Wilderfolk, but the cheers that went up would have bolstered Red into legend even if he weren't in the tale I tell you now.

The tribesman lay on the ground, forgotten at the feet of his butcher.

"Come on!" A voice jeered from the crowd. *"Can no one kill this man in single combat?"*

"See? I told you true." Giemar said. *"I bet you've never seen a Valforian who could hold his own against a Kharian."*

"Much less three," Knalc muttered.

"Who do you think is going next?"

Knalc already knew. He pushed his way through the crowd toward the man in red. As Knalc stepped into the arena he was surrounded by howls of encouragement, a handful even meant to bolster him.

The man in red remained unmoved, blue eyes staring at Knalc whose heavy browns blinked back.

A heartbeat passed and the cheers were choked to murmurs.

Careful as a fox footing through first snow, Knalc lifted his sword. He waved his blade, baiting Red to come to him. The man in red had done this dance thrice before that day and many times afore then. He knew better than to take bait freely given.

Knalc took a breath …

And dropped his sword—

And charged.

Red had not expected this. He looked at the abandoned blade and lost one precious battle-beat.

When he looked back to Knalc, what had before been merely the mind of a man's muscles became a mad attempt to salvage a single lost breath.

The Valforian steel stabbed at the spot Knalc's neck had been, but Knalc knew Valforian steel and how to outsmart it. He rolled to the ground, under the man's guard.

All the blade did was leave a cold, thin scar on Knalc's clay-heart.

Red had no time to react before Knalc seized his sword-arm

and snapped it in a single practiced motion

The man in red fell to the ground, shouting at the unnatural bend of his limb and the battle.

Cheers sprang from the crowd as Knalc found his feet again, a small smile hidden by his untamed beard. He reached for the knife on his belt, unsheathing the smaller Valforian weapon that had come within inches of his own life.

He bent over, held Red, and thrust the blade heart-ward—

"Hold!"

Only his honor-urge allowed Knalc to divert the knife into the blood dyed ground next to the man.

The order to hold came from Gamak Tols, the Gor of the Khar tribe. He, I tell you, was a Gor among Gor.

Knalc bowed.

Gamak raised his hairy hand in acknowledgment. *"You were going to kill this man—"*

"That was the purpose of the knife."

The gaze of Gamak stabbed at Knalc with all the intent of the spoken of weapon. Some legends say when Gamak was young and lily-cheeked he'd managed to kill the silver tip whose skin he wore with no more than the strength of his arms and the violent gaze of his own eyes. Bah, heed those tales not. Embellished legends that stretch beyond belief, I say.

"Do not interrupt me again. You were going to kill this man. But I have decided to delay his death. He has killed more of our tribe than any other single Valforian. It would be an insult to kill him in the same manner his brethren died."

"Gor Gamak," Knalc said. *"The soldiers we fought died warriors' deaths."*

"Yet this man is made of more than any of them. It is only fitting that we acknowledge this when administering his death."

A high scream came from under the wagon, the kind of scream you hear when a babe is shrieking for her mother.

A girl of no more than sixteen summers burst from under the wagon. Behind her, she dragged a small crying boy, whose feet didn't even have the sense to move while his sister dragged him.

Tears seeped from her face as she knelt next to the man in red.

The man—teeth clenched—looked up at her and whispered. "I'm sorry."

Knalc didn't move, waiting for the scene to end, waiting for the girl to throw herself onto the man in red and beg for her life or his life, or both.

The girl did no such thing.

Abandoning the boy, she reached out with slender fingers and pulled the knife from the ground. Fire reflected in the polished blade as she silently examined it.

She looked up at Knalc.

He was surprised when he couldn't spot distress or fear in her eyes. As it was, the look in her pupils struck a dreadful note in his own heart. In her eyes burned a bubbling, molten hatred.

"This is my mother's knife."

>>> **II** <<<

I TELL YOU ALL NOW, NEITHER sand nor sun holds heat more powerful than that between Knalc and the girl—a hatred that would have charred the soul of a less hardy man. Were they eyeing each other here now with us, the winter winds themselves would keep clear of our doors. It was only the voice of the mighty Gor Gamak that drove the scorchsome heat away.

"Bring these three back to camp."

The boy's crying grew moon-high as Knalc's tribesmen closed in. But the girl … she said nothing else. Even as the knife of her mother was torn from her hand and tossed to the ground, even as she was forced to her feet, she did nothing to resist. Her eyes remained on Knalc until she was dragged away. Even with her gone, Knalc felt as if her stare had singed him.

As soon as she was gone, Red was carted away and most of the crowd dispersed, leaving Knalc as he often was, alone under the eyes of Mamma Moon. If you could look unto him, most might think his manner akin to one of the statues left behind by the Old Ones.

When he did move, he and the world were older. The fires of the battle began to burn away, but the girl's gaze stung just as harshly as it had when she'd struck him with it. He retrieved his sword first, and then the knife that had been taken from the girl and her mother before her, noticing now the knife's pommel was blazed with an emblem of pronged lightning. As he left the slaughter, he found Giemar waiting for him.

"What is it she said to you?" Giemar asked.

"If you wanted to know, you should have listened."

"I listened," said Giemar. *"With all the ears the gods granted me. And I watched with every eye I had on hand. That girl was speaking Valforian, and you're the only Kharian who has a taste for their tongue."*

Knalc grunted and let his thumb rub the knife's handle. *"This was her mother's."*

"So her mother was the one you—"

"Unless the woman I killed stole it."

"Then what do you plan to do with her?"

Knalc looked up at Mamma Moon. *"Nothing. She and the boy will go the way of all prisoners."*

Giemar gave his friend a grim grin. *"I'm surprised."*

"Don't be. You know me better than most."

"You got a claim to them. You bested the man in red, and you wiggled your blade around in their mother."

Knalc glowered. *"I doubt she'd rush into my arms if I were to claim her."*

"So you'd rather let her into someone else's? Another Kharian might ask she open more than her own arms in return. More like they won't ask. And if that don't happen, you'd risk letting her run into the arms of Death?"

"When have you ever listened to your conscience? And why has it decided to pester me?"

*"I'm just telling you what your conscience would warn you, since

you lost yours way back."

Long behind them now, the wagons were crackling as the flames drowned in the cool breath of night. It cooled Knalc too, making the sweat and blood covering him solid and cracked, but it did not wither the memory of the hateful girl. He hoped by the time he returned to camp the part of his soul her heat had chewed on would cool. He hoped it wouldn't smoke-up his mind while he slept.

The two men trotted camp-ward and Mamma Moon watched their silent march. She had watched the two of them in the past, but that night marked the last time she would watch them walk like this. The silence that went with them was the comfortable kind that also moves with brothers standing over a spring kill, the kind that comes from clutching lovers hanging on the brink of sleep.

The kind of silence few speak of.

The two wandered back to the tent they shared—neither of them talking, neither of them having words that could muster more than less. After they were stripped down to nothing but bloodied flesh they dropped to dreaming.

It's said there's no sleep as deep as death, but when Knalc's lids closed each night he managed to get closer and closer to that great deep and still wake, and this night was no different. He was pulled from dreams the next morning by the screaming of his name, *"Knalc!"* shouted deep and guttural.

He opened his eyes and was blinded by daylight. He howled, *"What?"*

The light retreated as the tent flap closed. The world came back to Knalc in pieces as he puzzled out his guest.

"Damn you, Radruk!" Knalc stood, tugging on clothes. Giemar had already long left. *"That's a good day ruined by waking up to your ugly face!"*

Of all the heroes and whoresons you hear of—Alelex Who-Killed-The-World, Jundun Who-Slew-Seven, Thrandrun and Dooa—Radruk Who-Killed-His-Wife is one of the few who ain't never been drawn. As it's told by most, it wasn't his face, but the stink of his soul that left folks sour. It was the kind of wretched scent a mother wouldn't suffer to live unless her scent was twice as rotted, or unless her soul was so sweet it blotted the smell of his.

"I'm here about that girl you found last night," Radruk reeked.

"What about her?"

"As Giemar tells it, you forfeit all right to her. True?"

"True as breath."

"Good. Clothe yourself and come with me."

He was mostly sword-buckled as Radruk said this. All that was left was for him to pull his coywolf-skin cloak over his shoulders and smell the yester-scent of smoke and death clinging to it as he followed Radruk from the tent.

The camp was alive as any you've ever seen. More so. In those times the Wilderfolk were sparse and hard, and the Khar were iron strong. Not even the Quyn would have tromped through their territory; they might have hesitated to even pick at their discarded bones. The morning after a raid, the camp still bubbled with the revelries of night which had not died at dawn. Men and women belched laughter and fogged the memory of the night before with the pleasures of flesh and flagon.

Knalc did his best to ignore their hulubulub, trying to dispel dreams he couldn't recall. *"We're going to see the girl?"*

"Eh, yeah."

"Why?"

Radruk peered over his quickhatch-hide cloaked shoulder at Knalc. *"Since you will not, I am claiming the girl. You speak Valforian. I need you to tell her that she is to be my bride-wife."*

Knalc knew Radruk well and asked, *"Is she to be treated as well as your last wife?"*

"That's not a thing for you to mind."

Knalc walked a little faster. His innards felt something already gnawing at them. The prison tent began to loom. By the time they walked past the two guards at the tent mouth, Knalc felt a fearful bead of sweat running down his neck.

Inside the tent, twelve wooden poles as thick as Knalc's arm sprouted from the ground. A prisoner rested at the base of each pole; more than half were women—like as not, helpmates to be—a few were soldiers, strong of back, and if their wills were made of flimsome stuff they would make good workers. Nearly all were unconscious, and those who weren't were rattled by the agony of things missing and lost.

The girl and her brother were the only two children—unconscious. Radruk led Knalc to them and urged his clan-mate speak.

A hood of brown hair shrouded the girl's face. The bonds around her wrists were all that kept her upright on her knees. Her breathing whispered that she was alive and hinted she was sleeping better than she should have been.

"Well," Radruk said. *"Wake her up. I'll talk, you translate."*

Knalc glared at Radruk before muttering vague obscenities and giving the girl a rousing shake.

A parched groan creaked from her. Achingly, she righted herself. Hair fell away and she looked about the tent with fear-baked confusion. Boney muscles fought against her bonds. When struggling did nothing, she roared, a chapped and cracked sound. When she spotted her brother unconscious on the neighboring pole, she howled louder.

"Tell her I am Radruk and I welcome her to the Khar tribe."

"You don't want to ask her name?"

"We're getting married; we've got time to get to know one another. Relay my message."

Knalc cleared his throat, recalling Valforian flavor. "Greetings."

His single word crushed her shouts and called her gaze to him. Her mouth opened and closed, preparing a fresh scream which froze in its conception as recognition rampaged through her.

Harsh relaxation followed. A silence crueler than child-screams bore to him her anger's brunt.

He continued. "I am Knalc. This is Radruk. Welcome to the tribe Khar."

"Murderer."

"What did she say?"

"Good morning."

"Tell her that I will see to it that she is taken out of bondage before the sun has set."

"I have been told to tell you that you will not be here for long."

Fumes sputtered from her muscles, flexing and loosening in measured madness against her ropes.

"What did she say?" Radruk asked again.

"She didn't say anything, you deaf idiot!" Knalc snarled.

"Then translate it again, this time in a way she can understand!"

"I … assure you, you will be leaving soon."

"You killed her."

Knalc showed Radruk his hand and offered answer before a question could be asked. *"She said she's eager to leave."*

Radruk flashed a yellow smile. *"Good. Tell her that we will be married tonight."*

"My 'friend' wants me to tell you that—"

"I'm going to kill you."

Knalc faltered. Next to him the girl was swaddling sized. Yet, when he looked at her, the chest-chewing feeling of the night before returned.

At his hesitation, her lips went scythe-like. "You killed my mother. The second I am free, I am going to kill you." A stray tear punctuated her pale cheek.

He was unsure if he should laugh or leave, roar or repent, collapse or kill. It was a moment before he recognized the tone the girl used. It was one he'd heard before, one he'd once used himself. It was a tone used to make a promise.

"Well?" Radruk's voice cut through a flood of thoughts. *"Did you tell her?"*

"Change of plans," Knalc said. *"I've decided to claim the girl myself."*

ANY PRISONERS THAT MIGHT HAVE been bent to sleep were roused as Radruk took to cursing. If those Valforians could have understood what Radruk was saying, the weight and whine of his spite tinged tantrum would have beaten them back to unconsciousness. As it was, they were left to wake and scowl and groan and wince.

Knalc though, who knew the ill-wrought temper of his clan-kin's cadence, had already shut his ears and set to marching from that tent. Loathsome to be ignored, Radruk raged right behind him, leaving the Valforians bound and alone.

Though mutters and cries and prayers poured through those there, the girl just stared with silent anger in the wake of the two Wilderfolk. It was only once those beasts had left the tent that she allowed an unblinking trickle of tears to wash her cheeks. It was only once she was sure Knalc and Radruk were lost to hearing that she let a shriek-scream rend her throat. Grief-grabbed, she struggled savagesome against her ropes and they burned her for it. That burning loosed more tears.

"Bastards!" She screamed. "Heathen hellspawn! Damn you!"

Behind her, she could feel her brother, bound to the same pole, beginning to shake in fear and sorrow. She stilled herself at once and twisted to try to see him without reward.

At the tremor of his touch, her hatred cooled.

"Shhh, hey," she whispered sweet lies to him. "It's all right. It's all going to be okay. I'm sorry I yell. Are you hurt?"

She heard a single sniffle from her word-wanting sibling, which could have meant "yes."

"Are you hurt badly?"

Two sniffles seemed to mean "no."

She moved her hands to squeeze his wrist, the most comfort she could cobble.

It was then, voice as broken as his arm, that Red called out to the girl. "What about you? Are you okay?"

The broken man—ragged and blooded—was tied nearby, bound differently to most of the Valforians in that tent. He sat alone, a rope wrapped many times around his chest so that his back was propped up against the tent pole. Compared to his kin, he was comfort-captive, bound in such a way that a man with both his working arms could break from easy-like.

She stared at him for a long time, silent at first because she was unsure of how to react. Once she'd rattled an answer from her buzzing brain, she stayed silent to scold his witless-wondering.

He measured her meaning clear and put some use into his next ask.

"Have you seen your mother?"

This time when her silence came it wasn't scoldsome or smoldering. This time the silence—and the tears falling from her face with it—acted as answer.

Arm broken and bound by enemy monsters, the dread that had seeded in Red's heart the night before was watered by her quiet. The dread sprouted wicked and weedrooted as he drank in the sight of the girl's tears.

"How—" his voice was cracked as dead earth. "How did she die?"

Dull anger prompted the girl to try to wipe the tears from her face, shameful that such a man as Red would witness her crying for her mother.

"I don't know," she hung her head. "But the same monster that broke your arm had her knife. It's what he tried to kill you with."

"That … that doesn't mean she's dead." Red haggled with his heartache. "She might have dropped it. The Wildman might have found it. She could—"

"She would not. Lose. That! Knife!" She pulled again on her ropes, devouring the pain it caused. "That knife was given to her by her mother who received it from her mother before her! It's with that blade she taught me how to defend myself on the streets of Illmiv should the need arise. That knife was her last resort. Look around! Do you see her in this tent? I do not! But I did see her steel stolen by a mad man! You failed! You were supposed to protect us—to protect her! If she is dead, you ought to have gone cold before her. You failed your one job!"

As she hit the height of her shouting, the tent turned quiet as the few prisoners whose ears weren't clogged with sorrow listened.

"We've all lost, girl." Said one voice.

Said another, "Your mother, bless her soul, was one of the lucky ones."

Behind her, she could tell her brother had gone wholly to weeping while trying to hide it from her. Red was sniffling now, but he could use his voice so there was no meaning to be sifted from the sound.

In quick-time, Red found his words again. "Did your mother ever teach you how to handle yourself if you found a rope around your wrists?"

"No," her words were bitter as yarrow. "But you did."

"Did I?" He asked, maybe more of himself. "I suppose it's the same lesson learned either way. Do you remember what you were taught?"

"I do."

"Can you free yourself from the ropes then?"

For the first time, the girl pulled at her bindings with measured method.

She had done as she had been taught long ago without even meaning to, the lesson lingering in her soul. As she was tied, she'd kept as much space as she could atween her wrists. Most Wilderfolk know battle and blood better than binding, so even many of those who know their knots don't bother to tarry in their tying. Wiser now in her wriggling, she felt the rub of freedom in the ropes.

"I can," she said and set to steady work.

As she did, she thought of breaking loose and leaving Red to rot. Of running off with her brother and taking to the Wilderlands. Though sadness clutched her at leaving the other prisoners to the Wilderfolk, she knew they would be more noisome than necessary in the wild places of the world. Even those who might prove their worth in the Wilderlands would just draw more attention. Best to keep the escapees as few as possible, make it not worth risking going after two when ten or more were still secure.

Red must have guessed at her thoughts because before those musings could turn to mission, he said, "Remember to break me free once you're loose. I may not have my arm, but I can still be of use. I've been through the Wilderlands before."

Had he not been right, she would have left him to die just for saying such.

THOSE OF YOU WHO LEND your ear often to tellings in our halls know this to be true: tellers lie more than anyone else.

That's because they talk more than anyone else, changing tellings a touch each time; eventually a cloud-grey evening dampened by drizzle gets turned to a sky-cracking night drowned in rain and blasted black.

I'll confess to some stretching myself. Most are minor morsels. A slab of meat sounds better than a sliver, a shout hits the ear better than a simple saying, a quick death cuts deeper than a dragged and dreary plucking of soul from frail flesh. If you've heard me sing of the Great Stone-Licker, I've changed the tooth count of that horrid beast in my every telling—not just because ninety-nine might sound better one night and a hundred-hundred be better the next, but because I'm one of few who's had the chance to count the creator's horrid teeth and couldn't sure-say what the number is. Though I know that ninety-nine might as well be a hundred-hundred to the sorry soul caught in the chomping.

If you've heard other stories about Gor Gamak, you might have heard how, at fourteen, he slew a silver tip while wandering south. You would have heard about how he once stormed a Valforian caravan single-handed. You would certainly have heard about his lost left eye that was wizard-blasted before he berzerked and broke upon his knee the wizard's staff and spine in turn.

Tellers are a dishonest bunch who trade in mountain-made lies, but there's some stories we can't stack higher than they are.

I met Gor Gamak once, not long before he was honor-beckoned to the woods in his Death Walk. When I met him, he was *old* and had already crumbled beneath the rubble of his life. When Knalc and Radruk stood before him though, he was old, yes, and only half the highsome-worth of his youth, but that still made him more than near any other Gor from here to Hillwoe.

With patience, he sat on his throne of bones—made of the royal remains of every Kharian Gor before him—and listened to Radruk shout and spit in hair-tearing anger.

"This hellspit liar swore away his claim to the Valfling. But now, seeing her close-like, he's decided he wants to get pretty with her. He breaks bone and vow in kind, and men who care not for word nor blood in any part are as good as hungry coywolves waiting for us to go fat in trust. I say we turn the mutt loose into the Wilderlands where he can rave and foam with his own kind, where he won't eye the food of other men with hunger-lust. If we would let him have his way, he'd sleep-slay you, take your throne, and neglect to honor your bones their sacred right. He is toothless in his oaths and has too many teeth in his day-to-day dealings, he gives his word only after he has cut you gutless. He would kiss your cheek only so he was close enough to gnaw you bloody."

Gor Gamak trained his single eye on Knalc. *"What do you say to your clan-mate's accusation, Knalc?"*

"I got no notion to kiss your cheek."

"And all else?"

"Any truth he said, he said in shreds."

Radruk roared. *"Lies! I asked him if he had forsaken his claim and he told me he did. 'True as breath,' he said unto me. 'True as breath,' exactly! Yet, sore as it makes my eyes, he still breathes!"*

"Your say, Knalc?"

Now, Knalc wasn't one for wit or whimsies, but what words he had he knew well enough, and those he said he knew better still. *"Ay, I did say 'true as breath.' But what Radruk says he asked ain't what he asked."*

"See! Even now he is baseless and word warping! He—"

The Gor held up a hand and held Radruk in his eye. *"Let him tell it, or I'll hear no more of you."*

Radruk sewed up his face with a scowl and went silent.

Knalc continued. *"What Radruk asked me wasn't whether I forfeit my claim, but whether Giemar told him I did. When he asked me that, I said he told it true."*

Radruk started to bubble, but Gor Gamak held high his hand again to keep him from boiling over. *"Then tell us, Knalc. Why would Giemar say this?"*

"I told Giemar I was thinking I might swear off the two. He must've misunderstood me and told Radruk it was a certain thing."

"You two-tongued traitor!" The other curses Radruk spewed ain't fit to be spoken out again. Some say that Death himself was brought to blush by his cussing, and that when Radruk died he suffered twice what he should have—that's all tellers' stacking though, since any soul to walk near Death knows he has neither shame nor courtesy, and you need both to blush.

All the blushing that happened then was under the beards of Knalc and the Gor, until the Gor could mind Radruk's ramble-rave no more and slammed a fist on his marrow throne. *"Enough! We'll settle this easy-like now. Knalc never said to me nor you, Radruk, that he was forsaking claim. So Knalc, tell us now and here, true to breath—do you lay claim to the Valflings?"*

Knalc took a long while to answer. Not because he was letting his mind tinker, but so that he could soak up the spite foaming from Radruk.

"I'll claim her," Knalc said. *"I'll claim all three of them. True as breath, sure as sin, clear as the clay on my chest. Especially if claiming is what keeps them out of your sanguine fingers, Radruk."*

There are ghosts of slanderers and spouses who, if you dared to summon them, could list to you all the world wide things that Radruk didn't take well to: being lied to, being lied about, being served food too hot or too tepid—but as each can tell you, the thing he hated most was being told "no."

He reached for his sword so swift, some say even Knalc would have died had the Gor not been there.

"Hold! Radruk, hold! Strike him down and I'll rend you nameless. He claims them, as he said. If you want to challenge his claim you can do it, but he'll hold steel as well and you'll be in common sight of the tribe."

Radruk let his bloodlust lift, but wrath still simmered on his brow. His sword stayed sheathed, but his fingers chewed on the hilt like a starving babe at its mother's tit.

"It ain't true what I said about you," Radruk eventually said. *"Nay, you're no coywolf. When a coywolf steals a stray morsel from his starving kin it's to satisfy his own hunger. But you—you're worse. You'd snatch away mead, meat, or man, not to satisfy yourself, but to spite those who elsewise might have been pleasured. I will not challenge your claim, but by all gods—even them being dead or false—I pray that girl brings you more pain than peace of mind!"*

"That's enough!" Gor Gamak rose from his throne. *"Knalc, we'll go now to the girl and I will witness your claim so that none may dispute it."*

"I'll go too," Radruk said. *"In case Knalc gains sanity in the walk over."*

"You'll do as you will," the Gor said. *"Just keep your sword and tongue in check."*

"I just want to see the look on her face when Knalc tells her that he's claimed her. She'll lose her maiden-mind before she gives him her maidenhead."

"I said enough!" The Gor reminded. *"We leave now."*

Pappa Sun was well and truly risen when they stepped from the tent, stray clouds scampered around him; but he was not annoyed enough to burn them up and they were not rambunctious enough to blot him out. Though Knalc had known he would claim the Valforians, he still felt a bitter tang dripping down the back of his tongue, into his stomach, and slipping into his limbs. He was uncertain. He knew the service he was doing the girl in saving her from Radruk could not unmake the death he had dealt to her mother. He hoped at least to keep her alive to find someone to wed who would treat her better than Radruk. The search for such a man would not be long, but it was a journey he doubted she'd be willing to walk with him. She was a Valfling: he could demand that any man who married her give him enough material to survive comfortably through the winter—a cold and unpleasant prospect to him. And his half-baked plan for her was still twice as cooked as his plan for the boy and the man in red.

Pondering and plans were never Knalc's area, and had led him to wreckage before. He prayed that such would not happen again, but before he could muster so much as a morsel of a plan they were at the prison tent again.

He followed the Gor and Radruk in, spending each second dreading the next as he moved closer to where the girl and her ilk were kept. Knalc was so tied-up in his own grief that it wasn't until getting nearer he heard, *"What is the meaning of this?"* from the Gor, and laughter from Radruk. Something had gone awry.

"Ain't no claiming happening today," Radruk spat. *"Not when*

them as would be claimed have run off!"

Loose rope and upturned earth were the only indications that the girl, her brother, and the man in red had been there.

OH, CHILDREN, THE MINUTES THEY spent interrogating those Valforians that were still bound-up gave those that weren't a mile. Knalc was the only one who could prod them with words, and his Valforian was rusted. Them that might have paid attention to how the trio had escaped were too pride-sick to speak, and them that weren't courage-quenched enough to keep their mouths shut didn't rightly know what had happened save that they were gone. And all while Knalc was trying to talk with them, Radruk laughed and taunted. *"You done claimed them, Knalc. You're honor stuck to track 'em down."*

"They ain't been properly claimed," Gor Gamuk said after he'd ordered men to turn over the camp for the Valforians. *"Knalc ain't honor stuck to nothing."*

"Course, losing children ain't no new thing for him."

My, Radruk's laughing grated. Like flesh-famished flies, his jeers pecked at Knalc even as he lived. Now, most folk think words are just as harmless as flies—can't hurt none. Them folk is those that don't know how to wield words, or else ain't had run-ins with bog flies. Nasty things they are that swarm you and chew into your flesh, needling deeper than bone and laying dozens of eggs that hatch like fire. If the swarm don't kill you, the hatching will. And that's the way it is with words most times. Knalc had words and memories festering beneath his skin, aching to burst, and hearing Radruk word-rake him now made them fresh. Knalc was one of them that thought words couldn't do much to you, but he knew pain and felt it hatching in him.

He knew the girl being gone was no real loss to him. She'd rather have been dead than in his care, or else in his care and seeing to it that he was dead. Her, the boy, and the man in red being gone as they were could well have been a blessing to him. But he knew Valforians don't live long in the Wilderlands. Even for the man in red—steel in battle ain't the same as steel of soul. And with the girl … he thought about the fire in her eyes. She wasn't likely to let the Wilderlands best her, though the two she traveled with wouldn't be much help in surviving. Red might know a thing or two about staying alive, but his broken arm meant he didn't even have the means to pray proper. The boy would be dead within a week for certain.

"What a noble thing you did, Coywolf," Radruk jeered. *"All you done is take 'em from me so they could die somewhere else. The gods-that-are knew my claim to be righteous and they punish you now. It's their way of saying Radruk knows best."*

"Gods ain't saying a thing to you Radruk," Gor Gamak bristled. *"Knalc don't have no claim to them and nor do you. We've no problem."*

"I'll go to 'em," Knalc said. He stood from kneeling and started out the tent.

"Are your ears on backward?" The Gor grabbed his shoulder. *"I say to you that you don't gotta go! I say to you they are already dead, and if they ain't, they will be when found. New wives and men with broken arms ain't worth the sweat and heart-hurt. There are plenty of fine women here older than that one and any man could be broken-armed if that's what you're hankering."*

Knalc shrugged the Gor's hand away. *"I ain't hankering for nothing. Just don't want them dying in the Wilderlands—their blood might bring beasts and boars. Easier to bring 'em back here now than fight hungry animals later."*

Radruk was still laughing as Knalc walked out and I can't curse him, even with his twisted heart: beast and boars bring food and warm skins when they attack. Fishing Valforians out of the Wilderlands might get you a warm bed if that's the thing you're after, but Knalc had no eye for that now; it might bring your clan a slave, but Valforian slaves don't much last many camp changes; all Knalc could hope to gain were scars and hollow pride, though he had a hankering for neither. Now, most men who go alone into the Wilderlands bring food and water skins and ways of staying warm. Knalc had his sword and that's all he bothered bringing. He didn't busy himself with tracking. He didn't speak to anyone as he walked out of the camp—those who saw him must've thought he was on a Death Walk as he marched sword-straight into the Wilderlands.

Now, maybe you ain't been deep in the Wilderlands yourself, but you know 'em well just by drawing breath. Even the Valforians ahind their walls know the Wilderlands—why do you think they made those walls? They say there was a time before the Wilderlands, a time when no one but lonely man wandered the earth, where each man was a Gor over all else in this world, all manner of beast and bird and bushes were not things to fear. That was before Alelex Who-Killed-The-World angered the Green God of the Wilderlands by profaning his place as Gor over all-that-was. As punishment, ol' Green ripped the title from him and all men who didn't prove themselves worthy of it. Green then set to planting and watering faster than you can think to blink, sprouting up vines and iron-bark and bramble and blood-thorns and roots and dagger-leaves and told all the things that walked and crawled and swam and flew that they didn't have to listen no more to men, and Green gave them beasts all manner of tooth and claw and blessed 'em with a man-hunger so that they'd spill human blood to water ol'

Green's garden. And it was there Knalc leaned toward now.

He walked well out of sight of camp, through the ash and dust of the Valforian caravan, and let himself slump into the Wilderlands. Thorns bit at his ankles and branches stabbed at his clothes; birds with red and yellow eyes blared down from above, threatening to swoop at him on pale and black wings. There wasn't much in his mind while he walked. He didn't think, he didn't even move his eyes, he just stared forward, like maybe even he'd bought into believing he was on a Death Walk.

He wasn't far in when he stopped on a patch of ungrown earth and laid himself there. The eyes of the forest looked down at him and he slept, clutching the clay about his neck in his silent snoring.

The gods-that-are ain't kind to humans no more. There are those of 'em who don't got no strong fire either way for humans; but there are many more who want to see a world without us, the ones that splintered the souls of our ancestors on the rocks below Mount Hush-bee, and will try to do the same with yours when you die.

There is one god who has a pigmy liking for humans though: Grandma Dirt. All things come from her and each of 'em goes back, and 'cause of this she loves seed as much as cedar, and mountain much as man. Since Knalc had laid in ungrown earth, she could feel him clear and thought better than to let him fade into her. So, having some morsel of power over all that is, she set to shifting the forest, molding her curves so that the three lost Valforians would wander about to him.

Those three—the girl, her brother, and Red—had been stumbling and limping through the Wilderlands only a day, and were near ready to wither into Grandma Dirt themselves, when they happened upon Knalc sleeping.

Before the others could see him, the girl had sniffed him out among the dirt and grass. She didn't say nothing to alert the other two, but she lowered herself and began to slink away from them. Silent as sin, and wielding twice the malice, she snuck up. She stood and drank the moment for only a second before she was sight-seized by the knife on his belt. The steel was slight as a wish and cold as her mother's corpse—she snatched it breath-quick and pulled it back for heart-plunging.

She was stopped by the still-good hand of the man in red.

"Let me go," she said. Her muscles flexed and moved like hungry flames, but she could not rage free.

"Walls be blown …" he hissed, staring at Knalc. "I don't believe it." His tricksy steel dangled again from his belt and his broken arm hung in a sling made of the flaps of his red coat. The boy dawdled behind them both.

The girl tried to kick free. "Walls be blown! Sky crumble! Earth swallow us all! Let me kill him!" He took her kicks in shin and gut and groin, but she did not shake free.

"Dhorena," he said to her, "we haven't had food in two days, our feet bleed by the mile, and your brother can't take much more. I know you want to kill him. I do too, I might lose my arm because of him—"

"I *already* lost my mother to him!" she spat. "I don't care if it kills us all! He needs to die!"

The boy, hunger having long quieted his tears, began to poke at Knalc's sleeping body, unnoticed.

"We can see him dead," Red said. "But not now. Now we can use him. He knows the forest, and like as not knows the way back to Illmiv. I can't hunt with this damned arm. We'll take him prisoner and make him show us the way. Then, when we return, we'll see him on the less savory end of a noose. All the satisfaction of his demise without having to meet our own."

Her rage relaxed to merely a meager simmer. Slow, like a hunter untying a fresh kill from a net, Red released her. She nodded at him and he bobbed back, and she bobbed her head again and he hummed content—and then she body-flung herself at Knalc, knife raised high with wrath and hate pouring from her mouth, wishing to drown him in her anger before the blood-drawing began.

That soul-spit sound was what finally slapped Knalc to waking. His eyes drank in her and her hate; like any hunter worth his meat, Knalc reached for his blade.

His belt was bare, and he was just able to corner-eye that the boy had made off with his sword. In that breath, Dhorena was able to breast-bury her mother's blade in him. He howled and cawed. As she drew back, he rolled away.

He cursed and seized his sword from the boy just as Dhorena yoked more bosom-blood from him. The boy began to cry.

Now Knalc may've gone Wilder-ward to get them Valforians back but being waked by blood and steel makes men rabid.

He slashed at her, but she moved with rabbit feet. He grabbed at her, but she was fox slick. He charged at her, but found her blade bit fast as a thunder-snake.

He breathed and bled and looked at her. He spotted his red drooling off her knife and spotted an anger staining her soul and spreading in her eyes, discontent that red still ran life-wise through him. Knowing she was set to kill him, Knalc let his anger die and chilled his limbs and stared through her as she through him.

"I killed your mother," he said. *"I stabbed her 'cause she was doing same to me. She died on my sword. I have no hankering to run you through, but you don't seem to care."* This next bit he said in their tongue, a phrase he knew in Wilder-speak, Valforian, mad-tongue, and every language he'd even heard, words that make anyone who's worked up a blood-boil burst. "Your mother was a good fuck even after she was dead."

Children, Knalc didn't even know he'd been deafened by her scream until he heard his own ears ringing. Rage rolled off her. She heaved long ragged breaths. The rage that singed her soul now poured from her eyes.

True as breath, Death had seized Dhorena. Not seized in such that makes you dirt-rot, but Death had reached out a finger and struck her mind, putting her in a fever. You might have seen it before. When two people face down and one is caught by blood-fever, then Death will soon visit. Might like be the one who was struck, or just as like the one they're set to slay, but when you get struck by it, you don't slow 'til you've doubled killed the other—seeing to it they die and then setting to the corpse to make sure no jest-fueled gods could breathe so much as a blink back to their body.

And that's just what'd've happened had it only been the two of them: my telling would've ended here 'cause one of 'em would have died right then but for the fact the man in red still put stock in keeping the girl alive. Though arm-snapped and walk-worn, he and his blade snickered between the two.

Siiing! And his steel whipped the sword from Knalc's hand before it could sting the wild girl.

Siiing! It knocked the knife from her hand. And before she could turn her blood-fever to him instead, he slid away his sword and slammed her to the ground with his good arm. Her head hit a rock and cracked the fever from her.

Knalc's first thought was to break Red's other arm, but the man was ready for that. Soon as Knalc was within death-pace, Red's blade was tickling his neck.

The boy was wailing still.

"You shouldn't have said that," the man in red said. "About the girl's mother. You shouldn't have said that about Gloria."

Knalc growled at the end of his steel and spat. "Then … kill me."

"I kill you and I would fare just as well first putting the blade on the boy, then the girl, then myself."

Knalc did his best to ease himself to common speech and hide the way he was corner-eyeing his sword. "Should do … Easier than dying in Wilderlands. Faster."

"I know. That's why you will take us back."

"Won't."

Red leaned slight-like into his sword. Knalc's neck began a slow weep. "Will."

The wound was no worse than the painting the girl had just done on him. "Take you back? You can kill me there? No … rather die here. Now."

The ground-lain girl was moaning and rolling back to our waking world.

Red's eyes narrow. "If we bring you back, you'll have plenty of chances to overpower us. We're just a small boy, a brash girl, and a man with one good arm."

Knalc bobbed to Dhorena. "Will try to kill me … while I sleep. You have tricksome Valforian steel. Even broken, you are fast, more than me. Easier to kill me now."

Red grinded his teeth as Dhorena was near fully roused. "You sound like you want to die."

"Death better than your woman-whining."

Red leaned within a breath's width from him without sword-slaying him. "Then I will kill you here and we will go back to your camp, and I will be using my one good arm to drag your stupid carcass with us to show it to all your people."

The man in red knew that doin' so would strike Knalc nameless in death, and all his stories would wilt with him. Red also knew it'd mean he could be killed at once, but reasoned Dhorena and her brother might live.

He didn't reason wrong neither. You and me don't have much tied to life, and Knalc had even less. His sword and skin was all he had save his stories, shameful though they were. If a Valforian killed him, no one would ever whisper his name again—and much as some of his stories cut him, he couldn't bear the thought they'd stop; once you lose a man's story you lose all else, and oft times a man can stand to lose himself but can't stomach losing the things he keeps breathing, like children or tales of glory.

"You kill me, they kill you."

Red smiled. "I already died once. I don't think much of having to do it again. I'll lose even less this time."

Dhorena was starting to sit up now.

Knalc sniffed the air. He'd never seen an undead before, but he'd heard they smelled of burned blood and couldn't help but shed their skin so as not to be much more than sore muscles and crimson bones. Stories say their eyes are more vacant than those who are true-dead.

"You don't look dead. Not by what I heard. Not by what I see."

"A man dies many deaths before his flesh goes cold and some still afterward. My flesh hasn't gone cold yet, but I know the flavor of death."

"You want more of the flavor?"

"No, but it wouldn't sit poorly with me to have some more, I think."

She was groaning and her brother was at her side. Blood had made a nice mess of half her face. Her eyes were trying to find Knalc, but she was still stun-struck. "… you hit me."

"I'm sorry," Red said quickly, before looking back at Knalc. "I want you to make a deal with me now. You take us to the walls, to Illmiv, and we won't kill you here and now."

Knalc grunted. "Just kill me later then?"

Dhorena said, "... I'm blood. There's bleeding."

"We'll patch it in a minute," Red said, then to Knalc, "I didn't say that."

"But it will happen." He had a sense of how fast the man was, where the children were, and where his sword was waiting.

"I didn't say that. I did not say that."

"But it will happen."

Red sighed and rattled his skull. "I don't like what you did, and I'd like to kill you. I'd like to kill you right now. That's the truth. But I won't. Because you're the only one who can help us right now. When we get back to the walls though, I won't mind much killing you. But I understand what you did, you barbarians don't know any better than to do what your leader tells you, and you didn't realize who you were killing. I understand that. So—if you can lead us to Illmiv, safe behind brick—then I'll call all things even. The people where we're going, though, they won't see it that way. I'll say what I can for you, but they won't care to hear it. No one's cared to hear me for a long while and my words now couldn't buy a hand of corn. So I promise, I will tell them not to kill you, but if they do kill you to spite my words then that's no oath broken for my part."

"This is a kind way to say you will see me dead," said Knalc. "A cruel way to tell me I've been speaking right."

"It just works out like that. It's not much, but it's what I can promise. Do we have a deal?"

But Dhorena got to murmuring. "No," said she, through blood-rinsed lips. "You said that when we brought him home we'd see him hanged."

Red looked back at her to send her a scolding look, and that was all Knalc was waiting for.

He jumped for his sword. Landing dirt-bellied, he grasped it in his hand.

The boy cried. Red turned. The girl tried to find her feet but fell.

Knalc looked at the brother for just a heartbeat and knew he could snatch or stab him. Oh, children, he thought about it.

But Red reeled at him, blade-bidden, and Knalc faced the more fatal foe.

Without a look, he slashed at Red. His blade licked flesh—lapping up a wholesome chunk.

No sooner had he felt his steel dig deep than that Valforian blade, always cunning, slipped neat-like into his ribs.

He screamed and he roared and he cried and they fell and the world went black and red.

VI

KNALC HAD BEEN LOOKING TO slash Red's heart clean and beating from his chest. Yet the way Red had slung his arm—oh, children—that had saved his life. That arm offered something for Knalc's sword to slash that wasn't the man's chest. Knalc's blade had licked through the muscle and bone of Red's arm, leaving it a mangled mess, but Red's human heart was untouched.

For Red's part, his Valforian steel had lunged clean through Knalc but only tickled and bled the ribs, a place most don't keep hearts.

The encounter left both life-limp but for their breathing.

The girl had wanted to kill Knalc, she'd wanted to kill him with mightsome intent, but with everyone bleeding but her brother, she knew that Knalc might be all that could save them. So she and her brother had worked long and hard to drag Red and Knalc deeper into the Wilderlands. There, they built a fire to ward off cold and dark, and bloodthirsty beasts.

It was not long later that Red took to screaming and woke Knalc.

Upon unfastening his eyes and rising from his battle-rest, Knalc found himself rolled fireside (his bleeding clogged by leaves) and when he was able to look past the flames, he saw why Red was howling so. Such a slaughtering had been visited to the man's arm that Dhorena was having to slice him free of it.

She undid Red's belt from his britches and fastened it tight around the injured arm.

The man chewed fitfully on a rag but his screams slipped through while his feet did a pain-jig. With his remaining hand, he throttled a tree branch, wicked and thick, with such panic that blood was rung from palm-flesh.

Sorrowsome to say, the girl had no great strength. From how she hacked at Red with Knalc's blade, she knew how to handle steel; but from how she bit harder on her own lip with every scream the man let loose, it was clear she hadn't grown to stomach blood and wriggling muscles.

Knalc tried to stand, but pain frosted his chest when he made to move. He looked down and saw that he was slick and red and glowing in the firelight.

The boy was looking on, drinking from Knalc's water skin. Watching. Silent and no longer crying. Knalc licked ash-lidded lips, trying not to want for water.

There was a splintering and ripping sound. A curdling yorp and a flesh-thud as Red's arm fell to the dirt. Tears were in both Red's eyes and Dhorena's, their weeping dripped into the blood making it thinner, clearer, and more abundant.

Red looked at Knalc, and hissed. "Bastard born ... bitch son." Red's voice was already getting faint. He crawled to his belly and lay opposite fireside of Knalc. In no time, he was still and quiet as rest enraptured him.

What passed for silence in the Wilderlands fell unto their camp, the click-tick of bugs gnawing and singing while owls swooped on shrieking voles and beasts with front-set eyes and fanged teeth growled and sniffed and hunted—making no sound they didn't mean to.

So much blood had been spilled by them that was now lying in the camp that the trees could be heard growing. The roots had lapped up the spilled blood and longed now for fresh flesh as food for growing strong.

The noises did not distract Dhorena, tired and torn though she was.

She stared through flame and smoke at Knalc, lying there. Knalc's sword and the arm of the man in red were both still at her feet. She was gore covered and her hands were still shaking, but her baleful glare was untrembled.

Knalc looked back at her and spat and laid his head to dirt, staring at leaves and the star spotted sky. He didn't hear her come over and didn't know she was there 'til she was looking down on him.

He growled and shut up his own eyes from her and set to sleeping.

The audacity.

Not long had his eyes been shut when he felt a flame-stone in his chest. He chewed his own teeth to keep from shouting. Eyes still closed, his hands searched first for his clay heart. When he found it safe, he quickly searched for the pain bringer and felt the girl's foot grinding into him, plowing and stomping tender wounds. Each heel-slam and foot-thump were like coal splinters being seeded into flesh.

He let that pain sprout and spout inside, trying to keep it from bursting past his lips. That made her lean into him all the harsher. The more wretchedly he wrestled to keep pain down, the more passionately she pressed him.

He grabbed at her. He tried to shake her off. But he was wound-spotted and weak and couldn't do more than bat at her.

Finally, her efforts ripped his lips to lose a scream as mangled as his body and shattered as his soul.

She gave her heel one final twist as the last of the shout leaked from him, spurring a less than mansome whimper. This seemed to satisfy her.

Her brother finished the water in Knalc's skin and curled up for sleep.

Knalc squinted through tears and tremors, he saw the girl sit against a fireside log and, smiling content, she began to slumber.

She woke thrice through the night and wound-stomped him each time.

It's hard to total how long they were in that camp. Each of them were spent, either by cuts or sorrows or both. Some tellers say they lay there a week. That's hogshit. Ain't no beast in the Wilderlands that'd let humans stay in the same place a week without accosting them—even them creatures that don't eat meat would have nibbled on 'em thinking they were ill-grown plants. Just a day don't seem quite right though. They was so bled and bruised, moving after just a day would have been a miracle. Some tellers amend this through mid-meeting and say they stayed three days before leaving. Them's the dumb-tongued tellers. All who's ever been Wilder-ward, Waste-ward, or even bed-ward knows that after about three days your body gets water starved and can't go on. At most they were sitting two days. Not a minute more, I tell you true.

Over those two days the girl and her brother found a river and a rich water-bulb plant. The next thing Knalc knew was the taste of sweet water sliding down his throat like rain on cracked earth. His eyes flicked and fluttered, and he was able to make out the shape of the boy standing over him. He tried to say something and coughed, sputtering up some of the water he'd gulped.

He heard the girl's voice somewhere. "I wanted to pour piss down your throat."

Knalc didn't say such, but he knew that if they'd piss-drowned him, he probably wouldn't have noticed it wasn't water. He was so parched, he probably wouldn't have cared much.

"What stopped you?"

"My little brother," Dhorena said. "Even if you deserve to die, that doesn't mean he does. You need to be the one to take us back or we'll die out here. He'll die out here and I don't want to lose anyone else I love to this place."

Knalc tried to sit up again, still impossible but this time it was just because his muscles were fitful and held him down. His wounds, he noticed, had been well tended by Wilder-standards.

"Why not … let me die here?" Knalc managed to say. "Take your red man. Have him cut your way home? With fancy Valforian steel."

A scoffing sound. "He isn't going to cut a thing. He's had a fever since we made camp. Just look at him."

Knalc may have been back-stuck, but he could move his head and neck. He swiveled about to catch the man in red.

Pale and sweat soaked, Red had a cold shaking about him. The man toed the bridge to death even as he sleep-clutched at his bloody stump.

"We're best off leaving him for … the silver tips," Knalc said. "Miracle they haven't sniffed us up already."

"What are silver tips?"

"Beasts," he said. "Nasty beasts. Know your own scent better than you do after a whiff."

"We're not leaving him behind."

"Why? He your father?"

"My father's dead."

"Not because of me, I hope."

The girl didn't answer him with words or pain. And he didn't plea sorry for his slights. Back then folks didn't go sorry for what they doled; you can't fix flesh with sympathies or wish back whispered hate with words. Knalc wouldn't have gone sorry even if he'd known how. He was lying closer to Death than he liked and didn't want it to take him with the girl having wrung his failures from him.

Knalc asked. "What's your name?"

"Dhorena," said she spitefully.

He looked at the boy, gumming the mouth of his water skin. "And your brother?"

"He doesn't have a name."

"Boy must be seven-winters-old. Why no name?"

"He's mute. He doesn't have a voice, so he doesn't have a name."

Knalc bobbed to the man in red. "And him?"

"He doesn't have a name either."

"Why's that?"

She drew a long sigh. "He did something horrid."

Knalc looked long at Red who twitched and shivered. "You want to let him die?"

Oh, the moments that ticked away afore she answered. "No … for the same reason I don't want you dead. He can help me and my brother."

"He can help tree root. Worms, too."

After he spoke this she stepped where he could gaze on her. Knalc saw how the Wilderlands ain't easy on Valflings.

Her face was scratched from Wilder-thorns and her scuff with Knalc. Her hair—brown and rare as butterscotch—was in snake-twists and hedge-tufts. Her clothing, cotton shirt with a Valforian blue cloak and wool trousers, was blood-smitten. It was plain she'd tried to soak the sanguine out, but all that did was make the red fainter. Around her waist she'd taken Red's belt (tying a vine around his stump instead) and wrapped it twice-thick around her own waist. Her mother's knife and Red's tricksome steel hung from there, both yet bearing blood beads.

"You know how to use steel?" Knalc asked, though his very skin told that tale.

She thumbed the knife handle and smiled death at him; eyes patient now.

There's a place to the far south called the Green Fire Battle Field. It's told, back when the Green God swallowed earth, that two-faced Fire turned jealous of the conquest. So Fire aired-up and let its belly bubble, boiling until it was hot as could be stomached, then it belched up a black and red and yellow storm of flames and ash and ember as you ain't ever seen or heard of, trying to scorch Green away. Whether Fire was just spiting Green or was wanting to steal the pleasure of gobbling humans, it's hard to say. The sky turned sin-black as Green and Fire duked.

It was only when Grandma Dirt couldn't tolerate their noise that she slapped them both back into place. She told Fire that the Green God had gotten there first and sent both to peace-making.

You might know that abated battlefield as Man Stone Garden— it's the wrong name for it, but some false-names still say truth and Man Stone Garden was called so 'cause of the humans turned to stone in the fighting. Those souls were sent burning by Fire's belch and touched by Dirt to stop their suffering, though they were kept from Death by her doing so.

But now I'm weaving myself out of my first story. What I want to tell is that Dhorena had hot-stomached her hate for now. Letting it build and brew inside her so as when she spit at Knalc her hate would be so hot even Grandma Dirt couldn't hope to cool him before he was ash-dead.

"All Valforians are taught to handle a knife well enough to skin

Wilderfolk," she gloated. "My father taught me how to use a sword before he died. Which is why I'll be able to protect you while you figure out how to help him."

She pointed to the man in red, and Knalc gave a belly-laugh so hard he thought it might've further cracked his rattled ribs and ripped new wounds in him. Eventually, the boy smiled with his laughing.

Dhorena couldn't catch a funny spot in what she'd said. She waited 'til he was breathing right again.

"Are you finished?"

"Not half as much as him."

"That's the man we're going to save, or else you'll die trying."

Knalc sneered. "If I lead you back, if you know your steel, why save him?"

"Because he—well—no one deserves to die in the Wilderlands."

You must forgive the girl for saying such, she knew nothing of the world and didn't see which way the shadow of Fate leaned from her.

Knalc asked her, "Where's a soul to die then?"

Her grin grew grimmer. "A worthy soul should die at home, on a mattress, at kindly age."

Knalc had never been on a mattress, or in age, or of the kindly kind. He laughed again despite her smiling and his suffering.

"Laugh all you like," Dhorena said. "You won't find it funny when you die out here or when your spirit is eaten by the Goat-Below for pre-supper. You won't laugh then."

"Neither will you. Not when you die. Not when you're soul-smashed below Hush-bee."

She closed up her ears and the gods-that-ain't made her bar up her mouth and hiss. "Heathen."

"Cunt."

"What?"

"Cunt."

She loomed over him again and he readied himself for another kick. Instead, she reached behind her, pulling a water skin he hadn't seen from her belt. She shook it, so he could hear it sloshing and full of water. Slow-like, she uncorked it and took a long swallow. Once she'd gulped a healthy dose she held it out toward him. When he made to take it from her, she poured the leftovers over his hair. He jaw-gabbed at the spittling drops, but came up tongue-dry and gasping mad.

"We're going to find a way to help him soon," she said. "And you're coming with me. If you don't feel like you can walk, I'll chop you up into more manageable chunks and drag you along with me."

He roared toothful at her, but she had already stepped out of his seeing. Noisy and quarrelsome as an infant, he rolled, trying to find his feet. What he wanted to do was stand, snatch up his sword, and be rid of girl and boy and one-armed man with single slashes. That was like as not the thought that got him up eventually. He knew each time his arms collapsed or his feet slipped, that he'd gotten that much closer to a full stand, that much closer to wrapping hand 'round hilt, that much closer to being rid of the three problems before him.

'Course, even if he'd found his feet and gone for his sword, the girl was watching him. Sitting atop a log and watching him wheeze and whimper his way to standing, his blade under her boots.

It was almost a full sun shift before he stood steady, sweat-wet as a stuck hog and chest heaving like a dying dog. But he stood, and if he stood then walking was less than a hop-skip more.

"Good," Dhorena said, and she jumped from her perch easy-like. "Now you'll show me how to help him."

VII

THERE'S ALL KINDS OF THINGS in the Wilderlands—all of them can kill you this way or that.

Tullo, Kieka, Ghron, and Sool—you four know this well, eh? Two of you having lost lovers to claws and teeth and creature-cunning. One of you has lost parents to the unseen, ice-mawed monster whose presence we could only prove with the dead and the bloody footsteps it left leading north.

Even Ghron—with leg and boldness broken by a brash buck who danced until ice and branch hunt-halted you for the season—even that mishap proves the wiles of Wilderbred creatures.

Still though, there's a lot in there that'll help a body or soul if you know where to wander, what to search for, and how to keep from giving the forest a good blood-watering while you do it; and still, when that is done, you'd best hope you have the wisdom, brains, and god-blessing of a medicine man, 'cause otherwise you'll just die clutching your cures before you can render them. As you can tell by now, Knalc wasn't no medicine man. Knalc was nothing to gawk at wisdom-wise. Knalc didn't matter most times to most gods. Knalc also hadn't died yet, which meant he had some worth and skill in the Wilderlands.

Hobbling around as he was though, he didn't feel much more

pricey than the dirt he stumbled on. Some of his wounds started to pucker and drool from his walking. His feet were sorer than they'd ever been, his arms were stiff as branches, and the girl was having her brother carry his sword and trail behind them while she kept that Valforian steel trained on Knalc. He fantasized of taking his sword from the child, even though he knew the girl's hand would move faster to his heart than he could to the boy, so he kept his eyes on the ground—for now.

He was looking for a vein leaf plant, known for slowing blood and easing pain fastlike. There were other plants and roots and leaves and spores and bulbs that might have done Red better, but Knalc didn't know those well enough to guess them, and every salt-worth fighter knows that when you're lost and bleeding in the Wilderlands, the vein leaf is the surest thing to save your life.

The search was slow and Knalc's eyes were faster than his feet. He'd search a spot twice before he was able muster a hobble to the next spot to eye over that patch of dirt and plants. The girl didn't help much neither; she'd poke and pick at things, raising them up and asking Knalc whether they were what he was looking for.

"No," he'd say.

"What?" She'd demand.

"No."

This tromp through the woods made Dhorena bed-close with the Wilderfolk word for "no." It was only just afore sunset she learned the word for "yes."

It was at the roots of a green-ash that Knalc picked the vein leaf. It was small and all alone in that root nook. The herb's sprout-side and roots are almost impossible to distinguish from one another, except for red bits on the vine-leaves. Most times, the best way to prepare a vein root for the most good is to set the sprout-side to boil while you chew the roots, then, when the boiling bit's done, you rinse your wounds with the stuff. That way, even a small plant can take care of maybe five folks if you got a good medicine man with wise hands to mind the way you snip and cut the plant.

Hard to say if Knalc knew that when he put the whole of it in his mouth.

Dhorena watched him chew. Her cheeks went sun-flavored and her brow went bow-stretched as she figured the sum of things.

"Was … Was that the plant we were looking for?"

"Yes," Knalc said 'tween chews, slight spit splashing from his mouth.

She started to draw her blade, but he didn't mind her much and just said, "I cannot help him before I help me."

She leveled the sword with his throat. "That wasn't what I wanted you to do."

He kept chewing. "*No. It is what I had to do. I bled too.*"

The girl's brother aimed Knalc's sword at him too, shadow-acting his sister who said, "Not as bad as him."

"My bleeding is my fault. His bleeding is his fault."

"You're the one who stabbed him."

"He stabbed me, I stabbed him. Doesn't matter who did stabbing. All that matters is who's bleeding. Besides,"—Knalc spit some plant shards—"you cut off his arm."

The girl redirected her steel to Knalc's heart. He could tell just from the way the sword shined and shook that she wanted to skewer him good. He didn't snort or quake, just waited some while she tried to keep her hand from opening him up like a dinner-hog. Eventually the death-shine dulled and her blade went steady.

"Well then," she said. "Since you've ensured you're taken care of, it shouldn't take you half as long to find the next one."

He gulped hard the plants he chewed. "Can't find it if it's not there."

"Then hope it's there."

A scuff might have rolled about then as Knalc was starting to get a warrior-wind, and the girl was less girl and more Bloodthirst bound to flesh. But danger dampened them both, a danger the world has forgotten in the time since this tale's happening.

Back when all these things were still winding on, there were Wastelands—them patches of earth that Green didn't get in the first gulp. You can see traces of them still, in places where the trees ain't so high and the grass ain't so flush and the air is a godless green that burns the lungs to breathe and makes the throat go all bark-strip. Think me truesome or not, I tell you this: people lived there once—or things like enough to people that for you to eat one or one to eat you would turn the darkest god red.

Wastefolk they were called and Wastefolk were a strange bunch, I'll say.

Hairless as the blue sky, they were, with eyes as true-grey as a winter-morn, and fingers fit for the fine picking they did in the dirt they crawled out of.

They was led by women. True—I see the way you all eye me now—true, there have been many a female Gor who've done better than a dunder-lout with loin-heft, but they didn't pick their leaders 'cause of how they led or fought or thought or even looked. They picked women 'cause women were rare to Wastefolk, to them each one houses a goddess-soul 'hind their milky eyes—if you lived in places as cracked and charred as the Wastelands, if you found every fifth birth a female, if only half of those survived, and if you saw 'em able to pour blood and milk over parched earth from their own flesh, then you'd think every woman twice as true as the gods we have. There's a god you can touch and hear and worship— there's a god you can kill if she don't go likewise with your thoughts.

And there, not far from Knalc and the girl, was exactly that kind of god. Through shade and leaf she and her followers moved—

shouting in the jeers and coughs of mad-tongue, which Knalc knew less of than Valforian. This bosom-goddess was cloaked in yellow powder-paint with darker symbols on her head and arms, a necklace of ropes and knots around her collar and sparingly wearing leather near as bleached as her flesh. Her zealots numbered maybe ten and were dressed in kind, but with no powder-paint or necklace. The meekest of them were naked. The garb blended fine to the Wastes, but it was 'cause they were in Wilder-place that they saw her so fast.

"Shit." Knalc nearly slit his own throat on Dhorena's sword as he pulled her and the boy to the ground.

"Get off—" Her shout was shut up by Knalc's hand over her mouth. Her brother, though confused, seemed to understand the need for quiet.

The Wastefolk hadn't seen them yet far as Knalc could sense. Slow-like, he began to ease the three of them over to the tree the vein leaf had been nestled 'neath. And during his easing he managed to swipe his sword back from the boy. Dhorena—only just truly seeing the Wastefolk—didn't seem to see the sword stolen back.

She hissed to Knalc once they were hidden. "Who … who are they?"

Branches cracked and leaves popped as they thrashed through the forest. Closer.

Closer than that.

The children might not have noticed it, but Knalc started to hear the voice of a Wildman. Not one from his tribe. No, this one had a different spice on his tongue. Knalc knew he could understand his words if he focused hard enough. He did his best not to focus, but as they came closer the meaning of the words cut him.

"You bastards! Bitch! Bastards!" The man howled. He was dragged into sight, pulled by the bosom-goddess who coughed and jeered

back at him.

Knalc could feel what was yet to come and covered both the children's eyes on instinct. The boy didn't seem to mind. Dhorena shook his hand off. Though they were yet unseen by the Wastefolk, they had a perfect view of everything.

The Wilder-person they'd snagged had been painted purpled by a beating, bleeding black and red across the hungry Green. With a heave, the bosom-goddess propped the man up against tree-bark. She hissed something at him.

He spat in her face.

Her zealots gasped as they gathered 'round—stooped so as not to over-shade their god—their spears and sickles waiting for her word.

With god-grace, she raised hand to her face, palmed the spit he'd launched unto her, looked at it on her hand, and lapped it up, her milky-whites looking into his swollen eyes all the while.

Then, she moved her hand to her side. With a silver flash, his belly spilled.

He sputtered blood—it dribbled onto her face. She smiled wide and stepped away. Her children set to pulling him apart, painting their god in living blood to keep her fertile.

I won't burden your soul by telling you how they cut him up or how long and loud he went on screaming. When they were done, he wasn't more than bone and scattered flesh, and the Green was happy and so were the Wastefolk. Pale visages spotted red, they were god-shook in those moments: lapping, licking, lurching through the remains of the no-longer-living—in terrible baptism, they soaked their hands in what blood they found and pressed it against their goddess until she'd gone dusk-red in their reveling. Her form came to look less like living flesh and more like a cold ruby pulled from the precious earth.

The boy must have smelled the blood, Knalc could feel his eyes starting to leak under his fingers. The girl had gone as still as the tree—but her fear could be felt by Knalc next to her and likewise anyone else who cared to sense for frightened things. Luck to them, the Wastefolk were quenched on fear for now, and all of them were in rapture at their goddess.

Slow-like, Knalc started to move away, leading the two kids as much as he could—praying they'd be quiet and not rally any loose eyes to them. It's hard to say when they were all far enough away to start breathing right, but it was around then that the boy started crying loud-like. His sister let some soft weeps out a little later.

Knalc had seen such blood spill before. It wouldn't have been mansome to let tears shake him, so he choked on them instead.

They got back to where Red was still lying, still breathing, still bleeding, still as death. The children were walking on their own accord by now, the brother and sister holding hands, not caring to keep their eyes from running. Knalc had no hand to hold and didn't much care to seek one out; he chose to make his hands busy. He set to work on the charred-up fire pit, gathering Green's limbs that'd been shed and left dry and dead around them, and piling those he found in hopes they'd house a flame. After some toiling, he managed to breathe some life into the pit and rolled Red nearer, even while knowing that Red would die, the fire would die, the children would die, and he himself would die in the Wilderlands—though he couldn't say how many sunsets away from such a smashing any of them might be. He clutched his clay heart and came as close to tears as he yet had that day.

Dhorena gave an asking glance to Knalc; Red was still groaning, death-cozy as he was. The children watched him as they huddled around Knalc's fire. The boy pulled on his sister's arm and grunted, she shook her head. She settled herself by the fireside, eyes still focused deep on Red.

Her voice was softer than it had been yet. "Is he going to die?"

Though Knalc could see sun-clear who she was talking of, he still asked, "The man or the boy?"

She shot Knalc a look—burning, but not as scoldsome as before—and pulled her brother kin-close. He wriggled in her arms, pouting for a fuller stomach.

There's no true silence in the Wilderlands. Here now, you can catch in stray seconds where there's nothing in the air at all. In the Wilderlands, your ear's filled with coywolf howling, laughing-cat japes, titterbugs, and all the big-eyed birds that hustle about; the trees themselves groan under the wind and all specter-sorts brood and dig about in the night. Some, like Lord Long-Tooth and his Pale Lady, ain't but stories to frighten children, but the Skin Serpent, Unglog, or the Grey are all truths to keep the more mansome in their place on either this side of death or the other. When you hear foul ruckus rising from the night that don't sound natural, you can mark it as one of them. All said, the Wilderlands ain't a quiet place, so no true silences fell on Knalc and Dhorena, just Wilder-silence, which oft times is louder than I am now. It was the rabble of that silence that chipped and grinded her patience and played and fed the things she'd seen not half-a-sun back.

Eventually she spoke again. "What … what were those things?"

Knalc set his eyes on her and saw she was scared. This near-death romp for vein leaf had unsettled her soul. He wondered if he'd looked half as frightened when he'd first seen what Wastefolk do—he wondered if he looked half as frightened now.

"Wastefolk," he said, tossing a stray stick into the flames. "They're from where Green don't grow."

Her brother was already starting to get sleep-settled in her arms, eyes flickering and waning. She pulled him closer. "But what's wrong with them?"

"Wrong …" he tried the word on his tongue a few licks, trying to suckle a true meaning from it. "World itself is *wrong*. They're just in it. They're just doing as we all do."

Her eyes narrowed on him. "Maybe what you do. That's not what we do, a Valforian soldier is taught about what is right to do in war and in battle and—"

"World isn't right. Battle isn't *right*. Soldier isn't *right*. I've seen what Valforians do and I've named it many things, but never 'right.'"

Dhorena's fingers wrapped right around her brother's arm, almost shaking him from sleep. "It's a near sight closer to 'right' than raiding and raping and murder."

The fire cackled. "… Maybe so. But the gods themselves are not right. So who can say?"

"Well, your gods certainly are not right. Aprheus is the god above, the only god above, and he decides what is right and wrong. And walking among us is Pearlaphine who throws all worthy souls to the heavens to revel with Aprheus and those that have been evil and vile and wicked find their souls too heavy to fly up. They fall when thrown, banished under the earth and eaten slowly by the Goat-Below."

Forgive her, she didn't know better then and didn't understand that the only real gods be the ones you can feel and see.

"Gods ain't so kind as that. They shake and sway just as much as man, and all that makes them right is that nobody who'd call them wrong out-breathes or out-wrestles them."

Children, the girl even sneered like a heretic. "… You know I can't understand when you speak like that."

He shrugged, shuffling his foot through the dirt. "We're all going to the same place."

"Some of us. Yes."

He rustled a blanket from a bag the girl had stolen in her escape, then rustled up a second. He made like he was going to hand it to the girl and her brother, but as she reached for it he spread it over Red, whose face was moon-pale by now.

Knalc sat back down and huddled up in his own blanket. "Since we're both wicked men, best maybe to keep us warm? It's not long before we're in the mouth of the Goat-Below. You'll have Aprheus to keep you warm forever, hmm?"

"The fire here's perfectly warm, thanks."

"Hmm. Will you kill me while I sleep? For the blanket? For your mother?"

Red's sword wasn't far from her.

"No," she said. "Because tomorrow we're going to look for vein leaf and heal him."

Knalc snorted. "Can't heal a dead man."

"Then if you've held on to any, you might as well hand it over since it won't do you any good if he dies."

"*Goodnight.*" Knalc rolled over, not having the care to watch the girl.

Dhorena watched him and couldn't recall if sleep took her. But she remembered her waking dreams. How she imagined herself standing up in the night, walking over to Knalc, and running the sword through his leg and into the dirt so he couldn't move or run. Then she'd have taken his sword and cut off his arms to keep him from clawing at her as she sawed off his other leg; all the while a few of his own finger shoved in his mouth to keep him from screaming too loud as she went on to burn her mother's name in his chest with hot wood from the fire; and then claw out his eyes with her own fingernails as she set to ripping just one of his ears off with her teeth and set herself to jumping over and over and over and over and over again on his chest to see how many of his ribs she could splinter; and if he was still drawing breath after that she'd gather what blood she could of his and pour it into his mouth past his gnarled fingers and see if he'd choke to death on it; and even if he hadn't by then, she'd pull the sword from his remaining leg and start to work what she could on the limb and all else that was left of him …

VIII

NO SUN ROSE THE NEXT day; clouds choked light and color from the heavens. Blood still soured the air—it was hard to tell whether the scent was the bleeding of the Wildman they'd seen slain the day before blowing downwind, or the fresher foulings of Red's death-draining. It was this stench that sundered Dhorena from a sleep she didn't remember falling into. Her eyes flapped and she looked about.

Her brother was nestled up to her, slight and shivering at the morning cool, but safe. Red was pale as ever, looking already like a white-stone doppelgänger guarding a Valforian tomb. The fire had gone to ash, black as midnight, long faded. Knalc was nowhere in sight, only the shadow of where he'd slept remained.

Dhorena was on her feet, steel in hand, in a blink. Her heart whispered, "maybe he ran" and "maybe he went back to bring his clan" and "maybe he's waiting out there to kill you."

The Wilderlands cackled around her.

The heart-muttered "maybes" and the soul-shrieked "supposes" sent the girl spinning—eyeing every shadow as an enemy. The girl was right to be as frightened as she was. She was in the eye of the Wilderlands. In the Wilderlands, the grass itself would weave you up and drag you down if it could grow a touch faster. If bugs could bite a mite bigger we'd all be maggot-meat. All things held in the eye of the Green God long enough turn to dirt and dust, and ol' Green's eyes don't shut. This was the first time Dhorena came to know what you and I know surer than sin—the Wilderlands will kill you. All living things limp from it. Valforians try to lock their birth-roots 'hind walls and stone, but if ol' Green calls their names, they too limp off to meet Death.

Green is a hungry god, who all of us are birthed to sate. We all feed ol' Green, you, me, and the girl.

But not today.

As the girl spun and spun to fend off all the maybes reaching for her, something sneak-stepped her. She saw it too late.

She spun to stab—steel shining.

Knalc caught her sword-hand before she could slash death across his chest.

A shade of her was happy to see him; but as she shook off his hand she was thinking more of how to make a slow death for him.

"What are you doing back here?" she started.

Knalc reached to his side like he was ready to draw blade and blood. Instead he hefted up a fist of vein root.

The sounds had woken the boy and he stood not far away, watching, cave-mouthed with fright for what might happen next.

Dhorena squinted her eyes to see Knalc's purpose clear. "What happened to 'Can't heal a dead man?'"

"I woke-up. He wasn't dead," Knalc shrugged. *"And if he died out here, his blood might bring boars and beast we can't beat back."*

Dhorena looked at Red—corpse-pale and rot-breathing and with mayhap more of his blood slurped up by Grandma Dirt than there was left in his body. The girl had seen death before, but slow dying's a different thing. To see Death laze at his daily craft is watching a slow harvesting of the soul. Seeing the soul pulled from the body like a stubborn dyre-leech, not plucked up with ease but peeled from flesh and bone and muscle. It's slow and gruesome and ugly and ain't for watching. Yet she had been watching it happen to Red.

She knew Death was standing on Red's neck and she knew, more like than not in the Wilderlands, Death could be eyeing her neck soon after. Or more likely, her brother's.

Teeth gritted, she dropped the sword. Knalc let her go.

Each of the pair took the sum of the other, both thinking the other might make to mark them for Death. And neither did.

"Are you waiting for Pearlaphine to seize his soul?" She glowered. "Help him!" She stepped aside and sat, letting Knalc work.

Now you all marked my saying Knalc ain't no healer or wise man. But Knalc had seen some thirty springs and winters, and living so long in the Wilderlands don't teach you nothing. For better or worse, he'd stayed alive long enough that he knew what not to do.

Still, Red's wounds were deep.

Knalc worked the day away doing what he could. Dhorena just sat and watched. Sometimes she comforted her brother, who was going hunger-sick, but mostly she just watched, fighting the soul-itch she felt to take up Red's sword and slay his physician.

The Wilderlands grew around them.

The Wilderlands are always growing.

By the time the trees were swallowing the cloud-shrouded sun there was no telling what Death might still do with Red. Dhorena had done what she could to rekindle the dead wood of the night before, to warm herself and dry up her brother's tears.

Hands red as the dying day, Knalc heaved himself into a spot by the fire. He didn't speak, he just stared into the lilt-lit flames. In turn, Dhorena stared at him. Her brother stared at her, seeming to be searching for something in her eyes.

"What happens if he does die?" She asked.

Knalc went long without answering. Long enough that she thought he wouldn't bother. But he did speak. "If he does die, we dig into Grandma Dirt. So Wilder-things don't sniff him out. *Like as not there are already some sniffing up our trail.*"

"Why do you do that?"

"What?"

She creased her face at him. "That."

"What?"

"Why do you speak to me in a tongue I don't understand?"

"You understand enough."

"How is it that you speak Valforian?"

"Don't know."

She focused on him. If she needed him alive she would needle at him with words. "Did you do what crows do? Did you kill a Valforian and eat his tongue and learn his voice?"

Knalc laughed but didn't speak.

"I don't know how else you could have learned it. Savagery seems to be your sole skill."

Knalc felt the piercing of her words but shook it off like the bite of a sprout-snake. Still, he couldn't get himself to look her in the eye. He clutched his clay heart.

Dhorena saw this and tried to sink her teeth in deeper. "Tell me, do you get more pleasure out of killing women than you do men?" She nodded to Red. "Or do you just prefer to do it slowly with men?"

Knalc shook his head. "These words you throw at me for helping? I am … *healing* … the man."

"I don't know what you're doing to him. Maybe you poisoned him. Maybe you're preparing his soul to be eaten by your false gods. If so, you can stop. The man doesn't have a soul anymore."

"Why? Same reason his name was ripped from him?"

"Yes. Even if you kill him, you're not killing a man. Not truly. You're killing a coward. A deserter."

Knalc didn't look at the girl but at her brother who had started pulling grass up and chewing on it. "That mean the boy is without a soul, too?"

That question bit her back with the sting of a hidden sprout-snake attacking. "I—he…" She quickly covered her brother's ears. "He has a soul! That man had his name and got it torn away. His soul bore a title that was stripped from him. My brother's soul was never named and so it can't be taken."

Knalc laughed. Mocking-like. *"Sounds like hogshit."*

She paused and then she gaped. She understood enough. With a deep breath, she readied her word for wounding.

"You killed a woman because all you do is bathe in blood. You can't kill a coward because you are a coward. You haven't killed us because you enjoy the suffering of children. You want to wait to kill me until I'm a woman and you won't kill my brother because you don't think he's got a soul worth taking. I want you to know that when you try to kill me, I will fight you. I know my way around steel enough to kill a coward. Even if your steel is faster or sharper than mine, I will make sure each drop of blood you draw from me chokes you. Choke the air from me and I will ensure I suck the last ounce of air from your own lungs before I die. Every bone you break I will rip from my own flesh and plunge into yours. I might as well already be dead out here. But I will not let you kill me like you did my mother! I will not let you kill anyone else's mother. I will not die like—"

The Wilderlands grew around them.

Knalc was silent. The fire cackled. Knalc felt like it had gotten hotter—skin-scorching. Dhorena wished it was hotter so it might tear the tears from her face, her gaze wilted from Knalc.

Both wanted to wish the other dead.

One of them knew murder'd leave their soul-splintered and the other knew it would leave them body-broke. They came to quiet compromise—let the other linger for the time, until all ends were tied and bound. A contract sealed in silence with intent that blood would break it. This they understood.

Knalc spoke only when the understanding had settled between them. "Tomorrow we go back to Khar tribe."

"So your friend can make me marry him? Whatever wedding bed he tries to make for us will be the last bed he sleeps in."

Knalc gave a hearty, honest harrumph. "I hope you do. I have no love for Radruk. Kill him for you if I could."

"I'm not going back there. My brother and I are going home to Illmiv."

This harrumph was more humor-lacking than its predecessor. "You know how to get to Illmiv?"

"Of course, we just follow the Road."

This, children, was back when there was only one road—leastways, one road out where these happenings shook out. Wander west and you can still see it today—etched through those Wilderlands like a faded battle scar. The Road was Valforian dug with an aim at sending messages, traders, and food hither and yon. Back then it was a mightsome thing. At its widest point, twenty Valforian soldiers could march hip-close. Knalc knew the Road well—it was where he'd killed Dhorena's mother. He'd spilled more blood there than most anywhere else. There were four types of Valforians to tread on the Road: them with messages from city to city, them sending soldiers, them who are merchants, and them with travelers.

Messages, ink, and paper are as well as empty air to Wilderfolk. Soldiers carry that tricksome steel—good for killing, which means striking to steal from them is a good way to bleed yourself. Merchants carry fine furs and cloaks, but them is oft pompous-like and don't hold fast come cold winds—aside from that, those merchants made sure to bring a heap of soldiers.

The best for raiding were the travelers.

Pregnant with food and sturdy cloth, they had soldiers, yes, but not near enough to fend off a clan of Wilder-worth. And though they're travelers, them is Valforian travelers—sole-soft and shit-scared—not made for Wilder-wandering. They don't move fast, but slow and heavy, like a spear-bled boar. Of all the caravans, the Wilderfolk raided these most.

Dhorena told it true. The Road would lead them right to Illmiv, just as it was leading all manner of merchant and sort of soldier.

"Death is the only end on the Road for us," Knalc huffed. "Least that's how it is if we're found."

And Dhorena huffed. "One savage and three Valforians."

"Not as you tell it," Knalc said and counted their group. "You are one Valforian. You are one … nameless man. You are one boy. Mayhap they think I am setting a trap. Most like they'll kill us to be sure as not to be tricked."

"Better to die on the Road than live in godless land."

"Fine." Knalc stretched out his arms to show the Wilderlands around them. "I will trod back to my home. You trod back to your home. We will see who limps back living."

No more words passed between them for the rest of the night.

The boy wept for lack of food. The fire shrank for lack of fuel. The man in red cried for lack of arm. The girl and Knalc slept and did not miss the other's company. While they slept, the Wilderlands grew and laughed and lived and loomed around them.

IX

RED LIVED STILL WHEN THEY WOKE.

The days without food had taken their toll. The hatred and fear had fizzled out and left them all hunger-struck. The boy had it worst of all; he couldn't cry for all the water in him had washed away.

A spattering of words was all that was spent between Knalc and Dhorena.

Her, "Food?"

Him, "When we can."

And him, *"I'll bind some sticks and vines to carry him back."*

And her, "What?"

Knalc got to sifting and searching for vines and sticks. Afore long he had a shamble-craft sled and was tying Red to it. Blood-cracked, dust-mouthed, and gape-eyed Red was, but he wasn't hip-close with Death. Not yet.

Lugging his heft, Knalc bramble-bound him to his handy work and they all began their shuffle back through the Wilderlands— Knalc shouldering Red, Dhorena shouldering Red's steel. First they found a stream, they drank deep and leaf-spooned water to Red. Going further on their way, they plucked what scant fruits they could. Bloodberries, flyfruits, cherries, and treecorn. It wasn't no

Gor feast they found, but it kept 'em moving, which is all food is meant to do. Dhorena didn't lick a grain of anything until Knalc had also eaten it, but the boy didn't care. Knalc could have fed the child zealrounds, horse nettles, or virgin blush—the blush would have been the best way to end both the children; that five-leaf plant has a magic that'll turn the untainted redder and redder 'til they go flake-fleshed and start to rot alive. But the boy didn't know about virgin blush, and Knalc didn't feed him none, so the child was happy to keep putting every which thing in his gullet.

When they spoke, their words were breath-soft so as not to over-tempt the gods. Most of the speaking they did do was to answer silent questions. You know the way of children, even them with unspoken souls—name-hankering—the boy would point at anything strange to his eye and remain pointing until he knew its name.

"Eldertree. *Eldertree*," Knalc'd say in both tongues, even sprinkling in the Wastefolk words when he could find 'em. The boy would point and Knalc would tell him what what was. This was how they passed the day.

Pappa Sun had run the sky by the time they were nearing the Khar clan. It was then sour air filled Knalc's nostrils. In that breath, Knalc feared Red had run to Death. No, children. Death had not taken Red yet, but the scent was on the wind, mingle-mixed with the stink of ash and blood.

Knalc halted and held up his hand.

Dhorena, taken to carrying her brother, set the boy down in her halting. "What?"

Knalc breathed deep. "Do you smell that?"

"Everything smells out here."

"Yes. And I smell blood."

She squinted at him hard. "You said … 'yes' and … What was

the rest of it?"

"*Blood*," Knalc said. "Blood."

Dhorena took a hefty whiff. "It … smells like the night you raided our caravan."

"*Yes.*"

"*Blood* and fire," she used the Wilder-word, mayhap 'cause her own word would have made the blood real.

Knalc grim-nodded. "Stay. Until I know everything is safe."

He started to move, but steel song stopped him.

"*No*," she said in Wildertongue so she knew he understood, Red's blade in her hand. "How do I know this isn't a trick? Maybe you lied. Maybe you're good friends with Radruk and you're worried that if I fight when we get back I might kill you. Maybe you're planning on going ahead to bring back a party, so you can take me by force. Maybe—"

Knalc wound-up to laugh, but the dagger-look she shot him killed the notion. "*Fine*," he spat. "You want to risk whatever might be there? Then come."

She did, blade still set to strike. They moved on.

They didn't have to wait long to find the source of the death-stink.

Wastefolk ain't known for fighting.

With all the stones they got in the Wastes, the folk who lived there never could mold or muster steel. But what Wastefolk can muster is magicks—"gases" and "oils" if you want to use wizard blubjub. Their shamans and goddesses are the only ones wield-worthy, I seen 'em do it myself. Seen a whole city flame-swallowed. It was told to me—like I tell you this story—that sometimes Wastefolk leave camps and cities untouched by their scorch, yet still made men, women, and child dead in their sleep without even a god's brand on 'em. Once I saw 'em turn stone to dust in an instant and heard Grandma Dirt cry out.

From what Knalc and the girl saw, the Wastefolk were not of mercy-mood when they'd fought the Khar tribe. What a sight they left. Oh yes, Fire and Green long ago made their peace, but Fire knows it is a cold peace and will burn mightsome when spark-summoned to spite Green.

Where the Khar camp had been was now a scorch-puckered wound on the earth. Still seeping smoke and puss. Still smelling of flesh-rot.

Knalc—ears and nose and eyes and taste all sending pain through him—stepped forward. His foot sank through ash then earthy-blood. Clan-blood. Knalc fell to his knees, sputtering up ash.

He could taste it in his mouth. He'd never loved them—there were those he'd barely liked—but in the Wilderlands your aim ain't to like, it's to live, and Khar clan had held him just as he had held them. First he was sad that he couldn't tell the tang on his tongue—man or mutt or tent or worse—but not knowing was a mercy.

Blood had flowed so horribly here, even Grandma Dirt must not have been able to sip it all 'cause the sky had swallowed its share, you could see it streaked across the horizon.

It was hard to tell if anyone had lived or if all were burned and ash-buried.

The Wilderlands are never silent, but there was quiet there.

In that quiet, the tricksy Valforian steel got to singing tunes only Dhorena could hear: "Feed him to the grime and dirt," it mute-muttered. "A clanless murderer, no soul will mourn or miss the man. Bring justice to your mother by the steel of her people."

Knalc kneeled before her, not much different than Valforians do when they've done wrong and know they've done wrong and accept death. She'd raised the sword.

Two good chops and his neck would crack and tumble like a tree trunk.

Her mind had murdered him before her sword did—and her sword didn't get the chance there-then.

She was a breath from justice when a roar rippled the blood-soft earth.

She gasped and stopped.

Knalc was shook from his stupor, not even knowing he'd nearly been on his last lungful.

All of them looked to the roar, even Red—still dragged behind.

It was a silver tip.

A silver tip—big and brazen—lumbering into that scorch-puckered clearing.

Fear-faced, the boy pointed to the beast, not knowing its name, waiting for an answer from Knalc.

Knalc struggled to his feet, boots blood-chalked and heavy. "*Fuck.*"

Not even knowing what he'd said in Wildertongue, Dhorena spoke, "Fuck."

It took only a heartbeat for Knalc to know what the silver tip was scouring for. The scent of his burned clansmen had stained the air with the assurance of food—but the smoke-scent was an ill-made promise, for the fire had gobbled all the meat.

The creature was hungry and angry … and had caught their scent.

The silver tip lifted itself to its hind legs, standing oak-tall. When it fell back to all fours the earth shuddered.

"*Run!*" Knalc didn't need to translate for them to understand.

Dhorena scooped her brother up and turned to flee. Knalc gripped Red's sled and heaved him after. They ran, hard and fast as feet would let.

Their soles were sore from walking.

Every step the silver tip took was thunder.

The earth was sick with blood.

Dhorena slipped and fell. She screamed, and her brother toppled from her arms and rolled away. Trying to grab him again, she crawled back to where he fell.

The silver tip came like a summer storm, loud and lathering.

Knalc noticed Dhorena not keeping pace. He stopped and looked as she slipped. Then he turned away and kept going.

I hear some of you younger listeners gasping, don't worry. The man didn't make it more than four steps.

"*Shit*," he breathed.

His sword was in his hand then and snicked away the vines that bound him to Red's sled. He charged back toward the silver tip and toward the children, feet pounding through the blood and ashes of his kin to save a girl who'd kill him.

Dhorena got to her brother and wrapped her arms around him.

And the silver tip was on her soon after.

She started to stand and run again but saw it.

Huge though it was, the silver tip was faster than she'd supposed. She'd only seen it at a distance afore, she hadn't focused on the monster until it loomed above her. She had it in her head it would be big but this—

Thing about silver tips is, if you're as close to one as I am to you now, you don't really see the silver tip. You see morsels.

Eyes as orange as uggerfish venom.

A jaw sized to chomp you whole.

A hunger-hewn chest with room for you and three bosom-brothers.

A paw-claw which could crush a man's skull—a paw-claw that knocked Dhorena aside like you swat a gnat.

Dhorena felt like she was flying. She hit the ground aching, feast-prone for the silver tip.

As the silver tip loomed over her, meal-ready, she saw why they were called silver tips. The silvery hairs around their chest and shoulders—silver hair is reserved for the old, but silver tips are born battle-wise. They are fearsome and terrible and there ain't no shame in dying to them. If a silver tip wants to eat you, it has the sense to know whether or not it can, and if it decides it has means, gods help you.

Her kin-sword was at her belt but her arms were still sibling-saddled. Even if they hadn't been, no one sees a silver tip the first time and doesn't think that Death has come.

And Death would indeed have been there for Dhorena if Knalc had not been there for Dhorena.

A throat-parching battle yorp screamed from him as he flung himself gut-deep into the silver tip. In that charge, Knalc threw in the heart-bursting sorrow-wrath which was beating fresh within him. His mind was foaming like a rabid boar. His muscles rage-bubbling like fire springs. His scream, root-shaking.

In that assault, he put all his strength, all his fury, every drop of clan-mourning.

The beast was peeved.

Mighty peeved, yes.

But merely peeved.

Know it ain't impossible to kill a silver tip single-handed. As you heard-told from me, Gor Gamak was story-famed for doing just that. He fought such a beast under the eye of Mamma Moon, and under that orb drew its blood. But a sword is a poor choice for slaying silver tips. Arrows and traps, or spears as Gamak used, are best.

But a sword is what Knalc had in hand.

It was with sword in hand he was knocked down.

Yet Knalc didn't notice his ribs crack or the bleedin' cross his chest. He didn't notice much just then—not Red, not the children, not the blood soaking him—he only noticed the silver tip. 'Cause Knalc was going berzerk.

It's something a scant smattering of Wilderfolk could do back then. When their blood got pumping, when their brains were boiled in battle-foam, they'd berzerk. A warrior gets muscle-swollen to near twice his size and he don't feel pain or fear until he or foe is finished.

It had been a long time since Knalc had last gone berzerk. He'd kept it bottled up inside him, but standing on that field of death, he found that spark again.

He hadn't even found his feet before he flung himself at the silver tip again—steel flashing.

A storm of roars and blood and claws and it was hard to tell what belonged to Knalc and what was silver tip. Knalc met the beast blow for blow. Until he managed to shove his sticker into its gut.

The silver tip was gushing barrels, but that beast had blood to keep twenty men alive. To silver tips a barrel ain't but a drop.

"*Come on!*" Knalc roared, challenging the beast, his sword was still lodged in its side.

The silver tip's steps left the ground earth-cracked. Gaze set on him. Its maw went wide with breath like rot; sin poured from it—a tree-splintering roar boomed from 'tween those fangs. It chills my blood even in the telling.

It chilled Knalc's blood too. As he stared at those dagger teeth, at that death-pit, he felt the berzerk draining from him. Fear started to seep in.

I don't know how the girl did it.

Maybe it's 'cause the monster's focus was bent to Knalc.

Maybe it's 'cause Valforians have some unsung strength 'gainst silver tips.

Maybe she was just too stupid to be scared.

Dhorena came charging at the silver tip with Red's sword.

Thank the gods for tricksy Valforian steel. You use wild metals to beat at a silver tip and it takes three mansome thrusts to cut the pelt. But that Valforian blade slipped from one side of its neck out the other; easy as a snake through mud.

Death was already starting to seize the monster, but silver tips don't roll over easy even for their maker. The beast thrashed, one of its paws shattering the girl's leg-bone. She fell screaming and clutching.

Knalc took the moment and ran at the beast. Blade still buried in its side, he lunged toward his weapon, using all the might of his run to push the blade further down, widening the wound and letting blood flow from the beast like a red river.

Blood of beast and man mingled, but only beast was felled.

There came a final soul-wheeze from the silver tip as its orange eyes went white and Death left a cold handprint on that monster.

And then there was the living and the dead and, a mite away, Red somewhere between them.

The girl was still screaming over her broken leg.

Knalc was kneeling over the silver tip, breathing like a man near-drowned. He wanted to drive his blade into it many more times—to cut it up—to blame it for all the dead Khar that day. But the silver tip hadn't killed them. It was sun-clear the Wastefolk were to blame. And to stab the monster without aim would be a waste of good meat.

There was laughter. Dhorena's shrieks of pain had turned to laughter. Screaming laughter.

Her brother looked scared.

Knalc growled. "What you find humor in?"

"They're dead!" She proclaimed. "Your kin are dead!" She laughed. The screams of the slain rose up from the earth, but her voice stayed clear above them. "Now you know! Murderer! You kill and you kill and you kill! You dealt death. Suffering! Now all your blood wages have bought you is sanguine remedy! Ha! Ha! HA!"

Tears and blood washed her face and mixed down her cheeks onto her tongue as she shrieked. Salt and copper. A sampling of vengeance, a flavor she could take to.

The world of the living—Valforians, Wilderfolk, and Waste— is a world of salt and blood and death and earth anointed in ugly memories.

THE GIRL'S LEG WAS BROKEN. Not a beat after she'd shouted Knalc's sins heaven-high, she fell into an aching snooze.

Knalc made a camp he could lumber-lug her back to. Then he'd lugged Red. Then a heft-hunk of silver tip meat. All while the mute boy followed at his side.

Knalc didn't think as he took to toiling. He just did what he needed to live. He always did. When all was done—camp made and fire lit—he found himself shit-tuckered. Night had crept upon them; the boy was asleep, the girl still dreamed of death.

For a pitter, Knalc thought he'd stick them all. Bleed the Valforians in their sleep as he suspected his kin had been bled and burned in their sleep by Wastefolk. And why not? The three had been nothing but mischief and malice since their meeting.

But as I said, that was a pitter-thought. Knalc could swallow much, but he wasn't hungry for more blood.

"I'm impressed …" the faint voice shook Knalc from thought. If he'd been a mite more wake-weary he'd have already snatched his sword.

There wasn't no need though. It was just Red, fighting to stay awake—corpse-pale but breathing.

Knalc eyed him, waiting for more words. "Impressed?"

"Maybe it was just a fever vision, but I thought I saw you and Dhorena kill a silver tip." He nodded to Knalc's fresh furnished scars. "Seems, at least, that something failed to kill you."

"You seem slow to die."

"To my people, I'm already good as dead," he said. "Even more so now. Their mother is dead, I've failed my duty. Even if we get back alive, they'll kill me outright."

"I think the same would come to me." He knew it. He let loose a wormwood laugh as he thought on where they were. "Me, clanless. You, good as dead. The boy without a soul. A girl like to get herself killed. All alone in the Wilderlands."

Red's smile was missing teeth. "I'll admit there are more glamorous ways to die."

"No. There ain't."

"What's your plan? You could have left us for dead. You could probably find another clan."

Knalc pitched a stick near him into the fire-heart. "Seen enough death and blood today. *I didn't want more.*"

Red nodded solemnly. His eyes flickered like broken moth wings fighting to stay afloat. "So then, come tomorrow, what becomes of us?"

The Wilderlands waited for his answer.

Knalc looked at Dhorena sleeping fitful-like and got his noggin running. Death had hard hounded this girl. She might've died in the caravan burning. She might've died when she Wilder-wandered. She might have died at the Wastefolks' hands or the claw of a silver tip. But she was lying yonder, broken yet breathing.

Knalc wasn't no god-sworn man, but he didn't care to meddle with whatever kept Dhorena out of Death's tangled reach. He didn't want to see what consequences might bubble out of him seeing to her death.

Besides, youth death was a thing he'd learned he couldn't stomach even when he had to.

And she wasn't useless. They had been baptized as silver tip slayers together. Not as mighty a feat as doing it single-bladedly, but song-worth enough you're hearing about it now.

Yes, she was broken legged, but he was broken bodied—Red and the boy weren't much more than dead-heft for them to shoulder. Knalc had been in the Wilderlands alone before with folks worse than dead-heft, but that's a small story worth telling later.

"What's this city you were headed toward?"

"Illmiv," Red said.

"Know how to get there?"

"Of course."

"Know how to get there without the Road?"

Red hummed a moment. "Off the Road we'll die."

"Like as not," Knalc said. "Like as not Valforians find you on the Road with me, kill us all without a thought."

Red closed his eyes. He seemed to have slipped back toward death.

"Hey," Knalc spat.

Red didn't open his eyes. "I'm thinking." He drew a long breath. "You're right. Road and Wilderlands are just as bad, except they'll probably be looking for our caravan—looking for people to blame. To kill. They see a Wildman, me, and a boy without a voice, they'll probably kill us all. At least the Wilderlands won't be trying to kill us."

"Wilderlands are always trying to kill."

Red opened his eyes; doing so seemed almost to hurt him.

"Maybe so. But the Road is long and narrow and only goes two ways. The Wilderlands are huge, if we get deep in, there are paths that aren't just forward and back, left and right, up and down."

"I know," Knalc growled. "But if we wander Wilder-ward, you need to know: everything will be trying to kill you."

"I understand."

"So?"

"What?"

Knalc leaned back. "You never answered. Do you know how to get back without the Road?"

Red closed his eyes again. For near a moon shift he stayed mouth shut, eyes closed.

His voice cracked when he spoke. "Maybe." He nodded. "Probably. Back when I had a name and wore a different color, I was part of a hunting party that—"

"*Fuck*," Knalc groaned, word-sick. "Can you lead us there or not?"

"… it's south by southwest. I should be able to. Yes."

"Good."

That seemed to satisfy them both and each left the other to his thoughts.

But one thing was still wriggling in Knalc's mind. The whole reason they were out here. He kept circling to the fact that the one reason he wasn't in a nasty scrap that well as not would have been his end was that he'd chased after the Valforians. Not because he was noble or had some hero-swagger, but because of guilt wriggling.

"That woman I killed. Who was she?" Knalc asked, a question so soft he hoped Red wouldn't hear or be roused.

But Red heard and answered. "Gloria. Once married to the Mayn of Illmiv—and briefly Mayness herself—her family's had some wall-blasted luck of late. Her husband died and her son was born with no voice. She was the last of her family blood, the last of any old blood in the five cities, and all she has is a daughter to carry on the name. But that's to say nothing of what she was like—discontent, fair, angry, with a soul crafted by Aprheus himself. I loved that woman.

"And make no mistake,"—he opened his eyes and by some magic they were Dhorena's eyes in that moment. Pit-cold, unabating anger swelled and burned there, wanting to burst forth and strangle the Wildman. "I understand why you did what you did. You didn't know better. But if I were less sound of mind, if the girl and boy didn't need you—I'd eat your heart myself."

No more words drifted from that camp.

XI

HE WOKE HER UP BY snapping her bones back into place.

Her screaming would have sent a flutter-scatter of birds from the Wilderlands if he hadn't also cloth-clogged her mouth. For a mite, she kept trying to scream, trying to pull the cloth from her maw, but dropped back into a pain-shock sleep again. While she slept, Knalc made a splint of deadwood and vines and wound it round her broken leg. Then he minded the boy, fed him so he'd have strength to walk, and offered water so he wouldn't cry himself dry.

Then he set to cutting the silver tip into jerky and, when the boy took interest, he showed the child how to cut the meat—not too thick or too shallow—and how to treat it so it turned to jerky and not worm-rot. Eventually, he set him to it on his own. The child was slow, but it let Knalc go about the business of making bags and clothes fit for Wilderlands from the fur. Knalc had to chase off a few laughing-cats and stray coywolves who'd sniffed out blood and meat, but the Wilderlands didn't summon anything more horridsome.

Red and Dhorena slept most of the day. Red woke twice to get something in his belly. Dhorena woke many times, mostly to curse and spit, but she nibbled some and took her share of hearty sips.

Knalc worked through the night on cumber-craft clothes and bags, the boy tried to match him, but Knalc found the child drowsing not long after night fell.

By morning he'd managed to hamper together clothing for Dhorena and the boy and a bit of shoulder-wear for Red as well as some ill-made bags to carry what meat they'd managed to jerky-dry. There was still a mountain of silver tip meat left and Knalc was sad to see it go to rot, but knew he couldn't hope to jerky-dry it all—even if he could, they wouldn't be able to lug it all with them.

He worked again through the next day and it went much the same.

When the second night had ended, Knalc let himself sleep some too—or more like his scars and work and suffered-sorrows finally caught up with him and he fell asleep.

And when he came to waking, he found the rest had already roused.

He summed the others were waiting on his waking. Calm as moss. He smirked. "Didn't kill me in my sleep?"

Dhorena's hand went tight around the leather of her sword hilt, but no silver flash was summoned.

They started their leave-taking, got packed and clothed and road-ready. Red was more wakeful now, still exhausted and still needing to be sleigh-tugged, but at least he had crept away from Death. Knalc's joints were battle-sore and his body was tired from sleepless nights, but he managed to pull Red along and keep pace with Dhorena and her brother.

It was slow moving they did, but at least they had got to moving.

"By the Road we'd only be a week out from Illmiv," Red said—Knalc had to pull him hard through thick underbrush, roots and vine and crawling things snagged and caught him as they trudged. "Going through the Wilderlands though, I couldn't say."

"I don't know how Road-time turns to Wilder-time," Knalc said, yanking hard to pull him out of a rut.

"It's shy of two-hundred miles if that helps."

"Don't know miles. You know boar-runs?"

"No. How far's a boar-run?"

"Far as it wants."

Only the Wilderlands laughed.

"Wilderfolk don't measure distance," Knalc offered. "We walk a day and that's how far we walk. No miles, just how far we know it is. If I haven't been to a place, I don't know what it is walking."

Red sighed. "Then I'll do my best guess work. Say that by going off the Road we do a little less than double distance. That's four-hundred miles. In the caravan we did twenty miles a day. Out here on foot we can do, at most, ten miles a day. So with luck we can do maybe forty days. But accounting for delays—"

"We get there when we get there," Knalc said. "Or we die afore hand."

"We're headed south by southwest now," Red said, trying to keep a fight from stirring. "If we keep going this way, are there any dangers you know of? There's only one I can think of—"

"The River of Tears and Screams," Knalc recalled.

"A place called the Sea of Mist."

"Same place."

"I remember that," Dhorena said. "When we first left Illmiv we spent nearly half a day on a bridge dangling over a swirl of mist."

They'd all seen the mist, but none had been through it, and only Knalc had even heard tell of what happened in the Mist.

This is something I know none of you have witnessed, save maybe one, and I'd bet my sight you don't remember the horrors of that place—you were babeish and far away when you marked them.

The Valforians called it the Sea of Mist because that was all they saw—those who didn't build the bridge going over least ways—most just saw mist stretching out to the horizon and nothing else below. The River of Tears and Screams is what Wilderfolk called it 'cause, unlike the Valforians, they had to wade through it. Imagine having to navigate through mist and madness. Ain't no sun down there. Ain't no markers to tell you're headed right. Just you and whatever you bring. Mist is a small but tricksome god. Men can't walk straight down there 'cause Mist messes with their heads. Makes some see things they want or things they don't. Twists 'em up inside. And those who get lost in Mist ain't dead, but they sure as sin ain't alive. They wander through the mist and are likely to kill or maim who or whatever they bump into down in their white prison, doomed to never wander out. And as they wander, they scream: screaming at what they see or what they want or what they had or 'cause their minds are gone to rot and all that's left in their head is mist and madness.

The only cause for Valforians not calling it the River of Tears and Screams is 'cause they travel in wagons above it and most times can't hear the screaming over the rattling of the wheels and the easy chatting they make as they glide over the deep horrors. They just see the mist, and to them it's peaceful-like.

"I know we said we'd stick to the Wilderlands," Red said. "But the bridge might be our safest option. It's at the narrowest point of the Sea of Mist, so it only goes ten miles across. Even as badly beaten as we are, we ought to be able to travel that in a day then cut back into the Wilderlands."

"Yes," Knalc said. "But if Valforians do show up, then we're ripe for trampling over."

"What would be so bad about going through it?" Dhorena asked. "It's just mist."

"Then why did you build a bridge over it?"

Dhorena narrowed her eyes at him.

Red sighed. "In our own tongue, please?"

Knalc held up his hands. "I never walked in the mist. I never walked on *the bridge*. But if you want me to choose, I choose mist. I know of Wilderfolk who got past Mist alive. I don't know a soul that's ever walked *the bridge* and lived."

The girl gritted herself. "We've walked it. We've lived."

"It's different."

"What's your plan of action?" Red asked.

Knalc considered this. True, he'd heard tell those who made it through the River of Screams and Tears—"mist-walkers" they were called. In all the tellings he'd heard, no Mist-Walker was ever keen on jumping back in. Those who did weren't ever named Mist-Walker twice. Knalc knew there was god-scheming at work in the mist—from the Lost, to fog-toads, to Mist himself. But the one thing every storyteller sings of is the mist-madness. Not knowing where you true-tread 'cause you can't see sun or stars. Keepin' straight, he knew, would be the first-worst problem.

"We find the bridge," Knalc said. "But we don't tread over it. We walk its shadow. Follow its foundations."

Red took a spell to think that through. "Yes … yes. That's a good idea. You know anyone who's tried that before?"

"No. Not as far as I know. Most don't get so close to the Road unless they're raiding. No one raids *the bridge*, always soldiers there."

"Your idea is probably best then," Red said. "Find the bridge, walk under it, and hope for the best. Dhorena—"

The girl flinched. "You're not allowed to address me by—"

"There's no one here who can fault me but you."

She didn't respond with more than a nod.

"I was just saying," Red went on, "I hope you're ready to use that sword of mine you've been hefting around."

Knalc didn't look at her when she spoke, but he gut-felt her eyes boring into him when she answered. "I'm ready."

And so, they sauntered bridge-ward.

I won't flood your head with all the doings of all the days. They ate and slept, they walked and pissed. Ain't no flower tongue that can tell what happened in those days and keep you edge-chomping honest-like. I'm a well-seasoned teller and know better than to false-speak or waste your time. All you need know is, come the time they spotted the bridge, Red had finally managed to get walkin' again. Wasn't much speedier than a hobble though, which was good as not since Dhorena had weeks left afore her limp was like to heal.

A few times he took his steel back from her to see if he could make it sing again. A swing and side-snick and he'd draw a good hum from it. But his muscles were pain-sogged and he wasn't yet used to missing an arm, so he'd tire afore he could start a tune of worthy sort.

Inside three sun shifts they found the bridge.

Now, you—yes *you*, child—I know you've seen the bridge afore, or at least what's left of it. Same as you've seen Mist from far looking. Don't blush at me like that. I knew you to go poking places you were told not to. A hard-clung habit if you ask me. I remember when you were little more than a babe, running and whim-wandering for as long as you could out-wile the arms trying to snatch you up. I know you done seen what's left, and I know you 'ain't gone and forgotten that sight.

You seen what it is now, but I want you to imagine what it was then.

Stone and wood as man-made miracle, stretchin' a half day's walk and hanging over nothing. Hands of stone reached up out of the fog like the earth itself was trying to escape that place—they held aloft deadwood that stretched between 'em.

It's said the deadwood would be changed by Valforians when it came rot-loose. That's why the hands holdin' it were made of stone, cause stone don't rot. Many died making that bridge, and it's whispered that the workers wanted to escape the mist bad enough that those who couldn't find rock to lay would seize the bodies of the dead and build 'em into the stone that held the bridge. The stone don't rot, but bone and flesh and dead men do. 'Course, no Valforian has gone looking hard at those pillars since they were built.

"Is this the right spot?" Knalc asked, though he already knew the answer as they came to hill crest.

Knalc knew it must be right 'cause he hadn't imagined it half as well-made as it was. He was looking on it for the first time and had to remind himself this wasn't no god-feat, but mortal-made. Though he couldn't see how. The bridge was hard for the Wilderfolk to fathom—a wedding of wood and stone that held you in the air was too much, too much.

"Yeah," Red said. "This is the place." He pointed with his good arm to a far hill overlooking the bridge. "That'll be the guard tower."

Knalc had been so shock-fixed on the bridge he hadn't seen that distant peak. He was flabber-jawed, though tried not to show it. It was too big for a tent or a hut and, like the bridge, it was made of stone and wood and man's hubris. It was like the spine of Grandma Dirt had been twisted skyward.

"That a castle?" Knalc cowered.

"No," Red said. "Just a tower." All the Valforians kept their heads even. They'd seen these earth-torn atrocities before—they'd built them. "The guard they have stationed there might be able to spot us, but they'll mainly be watching for anyone who isn't meant to be crossing the bridge." He nodded at the rocky descent before them.

"With the girl's bad leg and with me still recovering, someone should try to find us a safe way down this hill."

Knalc side-eyed him, yet relented and started to shamble down the rock-smat hillside grumbling. *Lazy fucking Valforian.*

The girl waited for Knalc to waddle out of hearing before she took to whispering, pointing at the tower. "Abrum's Watch is right there. I say we let him try to find a way down that hill and make for the tower. There'll be upward of twenty soldiers there with food and fire. We go there, we rest up, and they can saddle us back to Illmiv. We don't have to stumble through the Wilderlands, we don't have to deal with the mist or this man."

The boy couldn't speak, but he understood enough. "Food and fire" he knew he liked and hearing his sister speak of them and point to a place in spitting distance made his eyes go wide. He tugged at the man in red's coat, pleading to go there too.

Red looked from the tower back to Knalc halfway down the hill. Then back to the tower. He shook his head.

Her hand went to his steel and he spotted it just as fast.

She didn't draw. Though her fingers hugged the hilt, his fingers hugged her wrist. The two of 'em were locked in their cold company for a mite of time. Until Red spoke again.

"Are you going to slay me with my own sword? Will that avenge your mother? Will that help your brother?"

She gritted her teeth and hardened her gaze. "Why?"

"Hmm?"

"Why don't we go to the tower?"

"Hmm." He pointed to the tower's peak. "There should be a flame at the top of the tower. The flame of Aprheus is required to be kept lit on all Valforian buildings outside the walls—the light of the civilized world—meant to scare off all those who haven't been touched by the protection of Aprheus.

"Now, it's most likely the flame is out and it'll be re-lit within an hour. Or, less likely, the soldiers posted here have gotten lax and it'll be a while before someone bothers to reignite the flame again … but we've already been attacked by Wilderfolk and those Wilderfolk were killed by Wastefolk. I can't see any sign of battle or siege from here, but given what we've seen we might have to assume the tower was taken."

The Wilderlands hummed around them.

Dhorena cursed. "So you think if we go to Abrum's Watch then there's as good a chance we'll run into Wilder or Wastefolk as our people?"

"Not quite an equal chance," Red considered. "But given what we've been through already, I don't like the odds. But if Abrum's Watch has been taken by Wilderfolk then our friend doesn't know about it or else he might have tried to convince us all to go to the tower."

Dhorena looked down the hill. Knalc was nearly at the bottom. "He might know. He might try to run to the tower as soon as he gets to the bottom. He'll get there and he'll tell his people where we are and then surround us."

Red watched him careful now too. "Maybe … but if he does, it'll at least be to capture and not kill us. If he wanted us dead he could have seen to that already."

"Speak for yourself."

He laughed. "I'll try to in the future … you've been conscious more than I have these past few days. Why do you suppose he's helping us as much as he is?"

"It doesn't matter," she said. "He'll help us, we'll get what we need, and then we'll see him dead. If he decides he doesn't want to help us anymore, then I'll just kill him outright."

He was quiet for a bit. "You remember how to kill a man?"

"You stab him until he stops moving."

"… True enough."

Knalc was back afore too much longer, bruised from a tumble or two he took while scouting. "Think I got a way down."

"Right," Red motioned. "Lead the way then."

Knalc hefted the boy onto his back. This—at first—scared the child, but before long he was clapping with joy. The Wildman led them shambling down the hill. It was slower going with Knalc having to warn of every bad step that might send 'em to a fall.

All the way, there was no movement from the tower.

In time, they came to the bottom of that descent—no more bruised or bloodied than before. As far as they could tell, no one had yet spotted 'em.

They weren't far from the bridge now.

As they wound about that rock strewn path, the Valforians saw almost at once that there were no guards. Gone were the bridge-keepers to judge-keep the bridge safe from the unsavory folk who might pass. Red and the girl passed a look between them.

To Knalc, the unmanned structure wasn't strange. The bridge seemed strong and sound enough to tend itself. What could men do to protect brick and stone?

They came near enough to hear the creaking of wood in the wind and smell the mist as it swirled and spiraled, unending.

"Here is fine," Red play hissed. "If we get much closer we'll get spotted from the tower for sure."

Knalc nodded and went to the edge of the mist-drop. He leaned over, looking straight down as he did.

I can't describe nothing to you, children. Do you understand me? I can't describe *nothing*. 'Cause that's what it was. Nothing. Just white. Spinning down there like a thick stew of rotten sort. Yes, it moved. Yes, it was and is. But all of it was nothing.

Knalc staggered back so as to see the world again—he was feeling fluster-headed looking down that drop. He couldn't see the bottom and he'd long ago lost any love for heights. He looked instead at the bridge; he was still thunder-struck that it hadn't been a god's work. By his eyes it looked new enough that it might have been built just yesterday. True, it seemed to float above the mass of mist, but the mist still breathed up and the bits that hung around the bridge were thick, and bit by bit they made it impossible to see on past the first hundred paces.

Anything could have been under that bridge.

"Walking under the bridge," Knalc said to himself. *"Not how I planned to die."*

"What was that?" Red called from behind.

"Nothing," Knalc said, then pointed into the mist. "I'll guess you still want me to find a way down afore we go so as to guide you?"

"Ideally."

Knalc grunted and grumbled again, "Lazy fucking Valforian."

He did as he was asked and found them a way down. It wasn't even a sun shift before they were all wading into that stew. Mist was the only god that knew them down there.

They sank out of sight and sanity.

That, I think, is where I'll end tonight's telling. We've got sinking of our own to get to, heading toward slumber or some kind of shut-eyed resting. I'll be up a while yet, in case our hunters trundle back in the blackest hour of night. Winterwind and other howling deadly things will be hot on their heels, like as not, and they ought to have someone to help them settle after their hard hunting.

Go, find your blankets and bedmates for the night. Come back tomorrow and I'll tell you what happened in Mist. I'll tell you about the Wilderlands' last wizard, I'll talk on Dhorena's trials, and dying gods and other terrible, terrible things. Rest now and we'll finish this tale tomorrow.

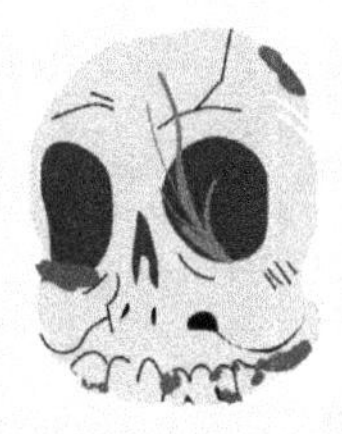

NIGHT TWO

XII

EARS! EARS! ATTEND ME NOW!

Douse your worrying and come close to the fire with what kin you can hold. Treasure them. Don't yet despair for those who were unheard from in the night, for they are a worthy sort who have faced many winters and, if you ask me, will face many more with a smirk as they recall the horrendous here-now.

Douse your worrying, and I'll weave you away from the here-now to a more horrorsome place: the gullet of Mist. That place Knalc, the girl, the man in red, and the brother all wandered into with the hope of finding Illmiv and avoiding death on the bridge above.

There were no gods that could hear them in that mist, save one. And Mist is a slippery sort of mischief maker, who's as like to leave you red in the face as dead in the dirt.

They went down down down into that sea of mist and tears and screams and loss, down down down until they were a crack away from Hell and all her horrors. And though they were lower than any low you ever seen, it didn't take 'em all that long to get there. Part of that is 'cause getting closer to Hell is always easier than crawling away from it. Another part is that Mist is always eager for more playthings and makes the journey faster for those who come to it.

When they did get there—so far into that crag they could hear the heart and feel the heat of Grandma Dirt—they realized something fast: it wasn't just that it was hard to see in the mist, but breathing and smelling and even thinking was a mite harder. The mist was more than just oppressive—it was smothersome.

They had no rope, but they used some strong vines that Knalc had kept from Red's sled to bind themselves to each other so no one was lost in that place.

"How should we walk?" Red asked as they gathered under the first pillar which extended above them to a bridge they couldn't see, they could only just make out the next pillar in the distance. "I think I should go in front. I may be wounded, but I can still hold my own for a moment and my eyes aren't so bad. Then we put the Wildman at the back. That's where an attack's most like to come from and he's the one who can best hold his own right now."

"Fine enough for me," Knalc said.

"Not for me," Dhorena piped. "I don't care to leave him in the back where he can use his steel to cut the rope without our noticing and leave us wandering in the mist alone."

"Why would I do that?"

"I won't pretend to understand your mind," she said. "I certainly won't pretend to trust you. So I'd prefer to have you somewhere in front of me."

They eventually landed on Knalc in the front, Dhorena in the back, brandishing Red's steel, and the boy and Red in the middle— the knife of Dhorena's mother ready in his one working hand.

And they walked along, passing column after column. But for some scars and scratches 'cross the wood and stone, they all looked the same. Knalc started growing certain that the columns they passed were not just the same looking, but the same single set each time they passed. Each pair looked to him identical to the last which started to seem same as the last afore that.

And they walked along.

Knalc started to realize he didn't even feel hungry. He didn't have a hankering for anything. Not odd if they'd only been walking for less than a sun shift—but mighty strange if it had been a day or two. Or three or …

And they walked along.

When he eventually tried to call back to Red, it was the first time he'd spoken since they'd started moving through the mist. The mist felt like cotton in his mouth. "You said half a day to walk it top side? How long do you reckon we've walked now?"

No answer came.

He turned.

White.

Empty mist.

No girl or boy or Red.

No vine-rope 'round his waist.

His steel was in his hand fast as you could think.

He spun, frenzied, for beast or foe.

He saw no beast, he saw no foe, he saw only a god: Mist swirling 'round him, breathing on him, groping him.

"Red!" Knalc screamed—his voice barely carried. "Dhorena!" so muted was his shout he wasn't even sure it had been aloud. He screamed a few more times to be sure he had even spoken. He heard no human reply.

He stopped. He planted his feet.

"*Dammit.*" He cursed himself.

In his frenzy-spinning he'd lost which way was forward and which was back.

The columns had been on his left, he thought he knew that much was right.

He let loose curses so long and foul that—had any other gods been present—they would have smote him for his profanity.

Left, he decided, he best remembered them being on his left—even if only by a notion—so that's where he would keep the columns.

He walked along—screaming for the Valforians with every step.

Only one god knows how long that went on for.

XIII

KNALC'S MADNESS WASN'T THE ONLY thing Mist was mustering in that moment.

The girl had been bringing up the rear of their ill-made parade, bound to the others by vine-rope and trust scraped from the refuse of sinister circumstance.

Though she had Red's worthy steel at her side in the world of white, she found herself missing her mother's knife. She knew she shouldn't, but the hankering was biting at her thoughts. Dhorena stared past her brother to Red's remaining hand, where the knife was ready-wielded. Shining with what little light there was, it marked the furthest point she could solid-see in that cursed crater.

"He should not be sullying that weapon with his hand," she said or thought. "It is a family heirloom. He can't be holding that."

A tiny voice—one she sorted as her better judgment, but might have been her brother had he had a voice—responded. "He needs it. He needs it to protect us."

She fumed. "He's failed at that over and over again. He abandoned his duty. He let his ward die. He couldn't even keep his own arm. Him holding that knife is impudence, impotence, and insult all at once."

The voice came back to her again. "You're the one who gave

him that knife when we started walking."

That managed to stem her steaming some.

Some clear thoughts came back to her then: she had given him that knife for their journey through the mist. He had failed many times, yes, but for all his failures he was capable and knew steel better than some souls know breathing. She was mad—mighty mad—at the man in red, but she did not hate him.

These things she knew were true.

So Mist laid a different trail for her mind to twist down.

"You don't hate the man in red, but you do hate the man who killed your mother."

"I do."

"The man who killed your mother is useful, but too dangerous to trust. The man in red might be useful, but only half as much as he used to be."

"He is. He is."

"You know the way home from here. It's just down the Road."

"It is … It is, but—"

"But soldiers might run upon you all and see a Wildman, a man marked by a red coat, a nameless boy, and a girl who claims to be noble but—if she is not recognized on sight—has no living parents to point to in proof that she is not some trick of the Wilderlands."

"Yes."

"But they might not be so merciless with just a girl and her quiet brother."

There was a wily sort of wisdom there she couldn't well refute.

And she didn't bother toil trying.

Red's steel flashed in her hands. In a single, silent stroke she cut the rope connecting her brother to Red and Knalc.

She pulled the boy close and covered his mouth. He startle-

struggled under her grip but she whispered in his ear.

"Hey, hey, it's just me, brother."

As she spoke, she watched as the man in red and the man who killed her mother disappeared into the mist with their ill-gotten knife. They were vanished in barely a breath.

"It's okay," she spoke quiet-like. "I'm going to get us out of here."

She grabbed her brother and turned and ran back toward where they'd trotted from. Mist mirthfully muffled their fleeing foot falls. Like rabbits running hawk-hidden, she moved low and fast and frantic, pulling her brother behind her.

Don't ask me how long they ran, I can't rightly say. But I do know that they only stopped when she heard him speak.

"Why don't you call me by my name?"

This voice sounded solid, no tiny thing bubbling in the back of the mind.

Her brother, she swore, had spoken words.

She stared at him, waiting for more, but he just stared at her. Face hard, chest heaving, a stream of tears running down his face.

"What did you say?" she asked, though his words were brain-burned in her.

And this time when she heard his words she watched his very mouth move.

"I wish you'd use my name when you speak to me."

Her body rattled, half with hope and half with dour dread. She shook her head.

"You … you don't have a name …"

"Would mom be alive if I had a name?"

"What?! What kind of question is that? No, she—the Wildman killed her. You couldn't have stopped that. A name wouldn't have stopped that."

More tears from her brother while salty snot ran over his lips.

"But she was traveling because dad lost his name, and we were traveling so mom could keep her name, and you have a name so we weren't worried about you traveling. I just thought that maybe if I had a name then we'd all have enough names that we wouldn't have to travel and mom wouldn't have to die and we wouldn't be here."

Now tears were in her eyes too and snot stirred behind her sinuses.

Dhorena knelt down in front of her brother and took his hand. "None of this has anything to do with you being named or not. All right? We're going to go home and everything is going to be normal again. Okay? It'll be you and me and … we'll figure it out. We have to. We'll figure it out."

"And will I have a name?"

"I can't give you a name. I wish I could, but Valforian law is very clear. You cannot speak, so I cannot name you. But we've got to keep moving, okay? We've got—"

The booming question cut her off: "Why won't you name me!" Yes, this came from her brother, but it sounded deeper to her ear than it ought. Though, as oughts stood, he still shouldn't have been speaking at all.

She let go of his hand and fell hard on her back and stared up at her brother as he pointed down at her and continued to speak.

"I'm speaking now, aren't I? Can't you hear me? I can walk and see and smell and smile! I can cry for our mother! I'm asking you—my sister—my flesh and blood! Please! Give me a name! Name me!"

A fear deeper than any she'd known sunk into Dhorena then. Yes, she'd seen Knalc and silver tips and Wastefolk—but here was a problem that steel and blood couldn't kill and that scared her mightsome.

Yet she answered still with steel.

A flash of steel and—screaming—she kin cut the rope still binding her and her brother together. The vine broke, never to be re-bound. She pushed away from him, still screaming, still crying, she scuttled away from the little boy.

He vanished to the mist in moments.

Frenzied, Dhorena didn't give mind to direction; all that can be said for certain is that she fled deeper into the mist. Alone, save for her memories and the ruthless warpings of the god of that place wrapping 'round her.

XIV

NEARBY AND FAR AWAY FROM Dhorena, no human response came to Knalc's own screaming. But while he ran his throat raw, a noise bristled from the mist.

Thunk... Thunk... Thunk...

Knalc stopped again and listened hard. This was not the heartbeat of Grandma Dirt.

Thunk... Thunk Thunk... Thunk...

This was a lifeless rhythm.

Thunk... ... ... Thunk...

Knalc wandered toward it.

Least, he thought he was going toward it. As he moved, the sound didn't get any louder, nor did it fade.

Thunk... Thunk... Thunk...

He started to see a shape.

It was a man—or man-like at least in height and frame. Less man-like were its movements: precise and reckless.

And Knalc realized two things: what the not-man-thing was doing, and that there was more than one.

Mist hadn't just turned 'em mad, but had made 'em either less or more than mortal man.

The not-man-things were gnawing, chewing on the foundations of the bridge. Clawing at it with wild, broken nails. Enough force in every bite that each chomp should have shattered their teeth. But it didn't.

It didn't do much to brittle the bridge either. But not doing much is a mite more than nothing.

As Knalc looked on he realized that a hundred of these things gnawing and jawing at the bone of this bridge for a year's time could turn the foundation frail. And then they could move on to another column.

Knalc fought off mist-madness to recall how long the bridge had been there. How many souls had been wrangled by the mist according to songs?

He didn't have time to recall—

The not-man-things had sensed him.

Children, pray a thing never walks toward you the way them things came to Knalc—wanting murder and not caring for thirst or pain or death.

One after another, they piled on to him, trampling over earth and kin in kind. Their claws reaching for him.

His blade cut through mist and flesh with equal ease. Blood and bodies fell and flew, melting fast from his blade and vanishing into the earth as soon as falling there. Knalc knew not how many he slew for none remained once he was done. But he roared all the while and peered into their mist-mad eyes with each slaying.

All of it muted by mist—violence and rage rendered near silent.

Time and number don't matter. What matters is that he slew 'em all.

'Cept one.

Through the mist a blade cut at him.

He moved without thinking and found his attacker.

A woman.

Like most Valforians, the woman had hands that ain't accustomed to holding blades or fighting off coywolves in the night.

In the moment he took to laugh, she painted fresh blood across his bare arm.

No longer amused, Knalc frowned. "Wait ..."

With a crazed howl, she pounced again.

Knalc stepped away. "I said wait!"

The woman's weapon hounded for him and marked him again.

"*Dammit!* I said wait! I think—"

She stabbed his chest—

Those hands were shaking now.

He screamed—more struck with horror than with pain as the woman rooted her knife around in the wound 'til its tip tickled his heart.

"Please. Stop."

With a guttural cry, she clawed his face—her fingers raking flesh. Drawing blood. Her knife twisted in his chest, watering the dirt.

Knalc felt no pain but he knew he had to act or die.

With easy wrath, he slipped his blade between her ribs, severing skin and lung and soul-stitching—reaffirming sin.

Blood slipped from between her lips and leaked down her chin.

She didn't struggle a mite.

"*Bitch*," he spat as he stood over her.

He smelled fire and ash and heard the screams of—

"No!"

Knalc turned, weapon ready, primed to strike down another not-man-thing. Ready to bleed another with ease and grace.

But it wasn't a not-man-thing that sprung at him. It was Dhorena, flying from the mist wreathed in steel and sorrow.

His battle-worn eyes spotted an opening in her guard. An easy gap where he could move his blade like needle through fabric—'cept he would be unsewing soul from flesh.

But Knalc faltered.

The sew-spot closed as she brought the blade at him and he was forced to weave away from her.

She landed easily, no regard to her broken leg. Like she felt no fire-throb shooting through her. She fixed one eye on Knalc.

Children, pray you never hurt a soul deep enough to make a body move to you the way she moved to Knalc—wanting blood and not caring for thirst or pain or death.

Her eyes had gone mist-mad, save for Sister Hatred in the one eye that followed Knalc, while the other—Brother Longing—looked back at the woman.

A small soul-sliver of guilt stung inside of him for only an instant. Then, suddensome, Knalc didn't know why he had faltered.

He who was flesh-render, soul-severer. Too many to count had long ago been unmade by him. His blade had gobbled the blood of hundreds and the taste was never varied or stale.

He roared—she screamed—they came at each other like blood lusting laughing-cats.

Each kept an eye for the other's heart.

Time and wounds dealt don't matter. What matters is that they slew each other.

In the same battle-breath, they each drove steel through the other's gut.

Knalc didn't feel the sliding of steel into his torso so much as he felt from the place of the blow that it was fatal. Wilderfolk don't die of old age. This was a day he knew would come. Rage and wrath withered within him. He felt no pain. He knew Death would come for him soon. Long since resigned to his end, he let the moment last, let himself live in the peace of his final breaths.

Dhorena deemed it not to be.

She twisted her sword in his gut. Milking pain from him.

Now he felt it—Knalc screamed as agony arched through him like lightning.

Though the girl had steel planted in her own heart—breaking through her back—she did not melt quiet into death. Blood seeped between her teeth as she twisted her lips to smiling. She didn't taste the blood. She didn't feel the wound. She just felt the pleasure of her sword in his chest. Heard the music of his death-yarp. Blazing with judgment, she leaned into him, driving the Valforian steel deeper, smiling wider. For a mite, that meant Knalc's sword was also driven deeper into her, but so seized was he by shock and horror he released his hilt.

"Death unto you who has slain my mother," she caroled to him— her words consuming him like mist. "Death unto you who has lost my brother! You have no grave. Death unto you. Your name is forgotten. Death unto you. Worms and fouler things will partake of your flesh and the Goat-Below will partake of your soul. Death unto you! And all of this is a better fate than you deserve for it is the fates you and yours have visited upon me and mine. Know that you deserve worse than this."

Knalc looked into her eyes and saw truth and fire there.

That was the last thing he saw as the mist closed in on him. His final sight was those two burning eyes. And then …

And then Dhorena felt his body go death-slack at the end of her sword.

She screamed wretchedly and wrenched the sword from his

corpse. A stream of tears scarred her cheeks. She panted heavy, each breath sending webs of pain through her. She fell to her knees and grinned at him, disappointed.

Wanting him to rise or shudder, to roll or shake so she could rob life from him again and again and again and again. She wished to flesh-bury her steel for every time she remembered her mother's death, her brother's face, until the quantity of Knalc's blood blotted out the memories. She cursed that men are killed but once.

Gritting her teeth, she grabbed the blade he had buried in her and yanked it from her own living chest.

She felt warm, then cold, then warm again as his blade fell to the ground.

She looked down at her clothes and saw that they were red. She laughed some. Red like the nameless man. Like Knalc, like her father, like her mother, like her brother soon, she would die in the Wilderlands. Her soul would come undone as easily as theirs. And she would not be mourned.

She missed her brother who had never known blood or brutality before this misadventure. Who deserved death least of any of them.

"I'm sorry," she thought she said. Mist glided over her and turned her world white, as her soul came untethered.

She fell next to him.

And there was silence.

XV

SOME STRAY FEW TELLERS STOP the tale there and spout that anything others say happened after that is naught but hearsay that wasn't never here nor there. Hear me say now that them who stop there are either fools or too tired to go on telling. Most like both.

It's as I told you: down there, Mist was the only god that knew them. Death was not permitted without Mist's beckoning. The blows they dealt and suffered were deathsome, yes. But Mist didn't have an eye to let Death take 'em. Tricksy Mist stitched up those wound riddled wretches and re-sewed their souls to their flesh.

They were lying there, all but corpses. Time ain't got no sway there so we can't number the days proper or even know if days passed. But were we there in the mist, standing over them, we would have felt a good mite older once they stirred.

The girl moved first. Sitting up and looking 'round—mist-madness gone from her gaze. He wasn't far from her but she had to squint to make him out: Knalc crumpled next to her. She looked at him and she wept.

Not 'cause she mourned his passing, no. She cried 'cause she saw him breathing. She cried because of all that had happened before: that her father could have abandoned her, that her mother could lose her title and then her life, that her brother could be lost in such a place and that she herself couldn't even revenge them, and that all other peace was lost to her.

The sound of her weeping is what woke Knalc. He sat and grasped his gut where he felt the itch of where steel or scar ought to be but found only smooth skin.

"You okay?" Knalc asked, not realizing he'd slipped back into Wildertongue.

She heaved and swallowed and looked at him, eyes red-run and spiteful. "Why won't you die?"

Knalc didn't have words for that. He just stood, picked up his steel, and kicked Red's blade back to the girl. *"Come on,"* he said. *"We'll find the other two."*

She looked at his steel but didn't move. "In the mist," she said. "Earlier. I was with my brother. I was with him and we were walking in the mist and I was telling him to be calm, that everything would be okay and then … and then he—he spoke to me—and it sounded like he was speaking with my father's voice. We were holding hands and he looked up at me and he said, 'Why have you forgotten me?' And I said, 'I haven't. We're here together right now. I'm bringing you home.' And he asked me, 'Why haven't you given me my name?' 'You don't have a name,' I told him. 'Why don't I have a name?' He said. 'Because you don't speak,' I answered, and … suddenly he grew and twisted and it was my father and he shouted at me.

"'I think! I move! I feel! I see! Why should you not name me? I writhe in pain when pricked! I wept for the death of my mother! I am asking you, here and now, blood-to-blood, to name me. Why do you deny me! Why do you deny me! Why—'"

She had to stop herself there. Chest heaving as if that very voice had possessed her to sputter such. Her eyes had a mourning mist to them as she looked about, suddenly seeing again where she was.

Knalc waited. *"Are you ready?"*

"Don't speak to me that way."

"What way?"

"This way."

He hadn't realized she'd picked up enough Wildertongue to speak like this. By my guessing, her learning that tongue by any measure was some Mist mischief. Still, Knalc wasn't sure how much she understood. *"Why not?"*

"I feel … trapped. When you speak like this."

"What do you feel trapped by?"

She pain-chuckled and held out her arms. *"All of this."* She laughed again, tears bubbled down her cheeks. She wiped the tears away and stood, picking up Red's steel as she did. *"I'm ready … I'm ready."*

Knalc nodded. "Yes. *Good."*

The fight had gone cold in both of them as they moved through fog and fear with weapons drawn but not aimed at the other's heart. They kept their eyes trained for more of the mist-mad. They kept their minds strained to keep out mischief. They kept their feet ready to leap. During this walk, for the first time, they didn't think on what would happen if the other tried to sudden-stab them. They both knew.

There came a bit as they wandered where the mist began to grow thinner and thinner. It never went away, but it got thin enough that they were able to see something horridsome.

Wood and stone strewn 'cross the ground like the soul-shattered under Hush-bee Mountain. It was more like a slain beast than a broken contraption of man. Four columns were crumpled there 'longside 'em. Chewed threw. Standing in front of the broken bridge were two shapes.

Knalc approached, prepared for fighting not-man-things, ready to stave off mist-madness. Mist was in an odd mood to not have him do so.

It was Red and the boy waiting there. Both of 'em awe-shook by the rubble and ruin of the bridge afore them.

"Brother!" Dhorena ran to him but stopped short of taking the boy up in her arms. She remembered how she'd last seen him and he her, had that truly been either of them. Her tongue itched, wringing for a name to call him. Then she noticed the broken bridge.

"What does this mean?" Knalc asked.

Red never moved his gaze from the wreckage. "It means that the power of Valforians doesn't run as deep as I thought it did … and doesn't hold as long as we've been lead to believe."

The idea that Mist could chew and rake and rip its way out of that pit would shiver any man's spine. The thought that Mist could chew and take and rip until our world crumbled into it was twice as fearsome a thought. Can you imagine that, child? A world made only of mist and madness? I bet you can. With more ease than them leastways.

"You remember making your way to this spot just now?" Red asked.

Dhorena hesitated. "We … we were walking …"

"*Yes*," Knalc said. "We remember."

The boy was silent. He watched his sister.

Red watched the wreckage of the world that'd cast him out. "I remember us all walking and then suddenly I was here … Don't know how long I've been here."

"Something happened to us," Knalc said. "I was walking and—"

"And he saw the bridge," Dhorena said. "We both did. That's how we got here. Same as you."

The boy was silent.

"We're nearly out at least," Red said, pointing at a yellow-marked bar of wood festering with the rest of the fallen portion of the bridge. "Assuming this section fell straight down, we're only two miles from the other side."

Knalc grunted. "Is that close?"

"Close enough. Come on."

They moved, leaving behind that heap of cracked wood and smashed stone. Those long dead had built the bridge—and if Valforian hands were ever called to fix it, then many who might have lived would know Death. But many more would only know Mist.

I won't bother you with how the rest of their walking went. A teller oughta share all she can, but not if it would turn to tedium.

Know they walked.

Know there was danger.

Know they conquered it, no worse weathered than before.

Know that you ain't got to know it, 'cause they hardly remembered it once they were through themselves.

Know they seemed to reach the other side.

They started to climb out. Out of the mist and away from Hell and horror. Hands, shaking and sweating, hefting themselves out of that god-stew. More than once, a finger slipped—more than once, one hand had to offer help to another. Red, with his single arm, fought harder than any to yank himself from that place. But none of them fell. None took that tumble.

Knalc pulled himself out.

Dhorena pulled herself out.

Red pulled himself out.

The boy was clinging to the rock face, struggling with his last few grasps. He looked up, coughing and whimpering for help.

Dhorena got down on her belly and crawled edge-ward.

"Brother!" she shouted—no name for the boy. "Grab my hand!"

Some say he fell.

He didn't.

She reached for his hand—aching to pull her kin from that horridsome stew—and he reached back. When their hands met, his palm and fingers turned to mist and steam. She screamed and grabbed to pull him up by his chest, his arms, his head—all turned to fog in her fingers.

She screamed and screamed and screamed and grabbed for him … but there was nothing left. Only mist and memory. She tried to throw herself back into the sea to find him—Knalc had to pin her to keep her from flinging herself over. She screamed and screamed and screamed and grabbed for nothing. Her tongue itched and wept to sing his name but had none to call him back by. It broke her heart to know she'd never hear his voice again. It cracked her soul to think she never had. She screamed and screamed and screamed and screamed, but had no name to shout for him, and even if she had, the boy himself would not have known it. She wailed and wailed for all she had lost to mist and memory.

XVI

THERE WAS NO NAME TO be etched on the stone and no body to build an earth-bed for. They stayed near the cliff edge, hoping to see the boy climbing back out of mist. They saw no such thing.

Dhorena did not speak. Knalc did not speak. As if the boy's death had passed his tonguelessness to them.

Only Red, teary with the loss of his second charge in short time, seemed able to make use of his words.

"I always thought he should have been called Amok," Red sorrow-whispered that night. "I know the Wilderfolk don't much mark their fallen, but Valforians do. To remember. I know it won't mean … much. But I can't leave his maker blank."

Single-armed and sorrow-riddled, Red took to finding a stone, smooth and flat to mark a lost soul. No small struggle was it for him, wrestling with one hand, to hold the stone and name-chisel it, but he did. He fought with earth and rock to find a place to plant the marker—but he found a place.

You all could go and see it now if you don't believe me. Run over water and land out to the west and you can see it. A stone that reads "Amok"—under the name in Valforian it reads, "A worthy son and blessed brother." Some two-tongued traveler must have come by it, 'cause below it you can read the same thing in Wilder-speak for all it's worth. Wilderfolk don't have a written tongue so all it means is folks who know those Valforian doodles can make sounds like the Wildertongue.

When Red came back, neither Knalc nor Dhorena had set a fire for warmth. Knalc was curled in his skins, sleeping. Dhorena was sitting near the edge and looking down after her brother. Later in life, when she learned that Mist was the god of his domain, she would wonder if Pearlaphine would be able to pass through to seize her brother's soul, and she wondered if even Pearlaphine could fling it high enough to escape that horridsome pit. She didn't dare wonder what would happen if his soul couldn't arch out of there. She didn't dare think that the Vox were right and he had no soul to fling.

Before he bedded for the night, Red rested his hand on her shoulder and was there. Just there. Existing next to her—you little realize how little you exist next to others. Afore long, he laid his head down. She did not.

Pappa Sun was hateful in his coming the next morning. Seeing their loss in garish gleam, seeing the night-black burned away to show the boy had not returned, dealt the cruelest wound—though not the last.

Knalc and Dhorena were still silent. Red had to rouse them from the camp.

"We need to move," he said. "We're too near the Road and the bridge. The Valforians might not yet know the bridge is split, but they will before long. When they do, there will be soldiers and mud-hounds sniffing through these woods. I don't want to be here to have to explain and I'd care even less to take the blame for it."

"Was the bridge really like that?" Dhorena's voice was flavor-flat. "It was down in the mist. We saw a lot of things down there I don't think were true."

Red tossed a bag to Knalc and another to her. "True or not, our six eyes saw it and we need to assume that any more that go that way will see the same. We can't afford to be here when someone comes looking."

Knalc grumbled some Wilder-curse but found his feet. Dhorena just looked at the palm of her hand that had failed her brother. "Do you think he was really walking that final stretch with us? Do you think he made the climb? Or—"

"Don't," Red said.

"Do you think br— Amok, really turned to mist in my hand at the whim of some cruel god?"

"Dhorena—"

"Or do you think we lost him not long after we first descended? Do you think he's still down there—scared and suffering and …"

"Mist-Walkers," Knalc said. "Mist-Walkers is what we are now. There ain't no going back to him. Mist-Walkers only walk once. All those who try again get lost." He waited for her to look at him before he went on. He waited more than a mite, but she looked. "We both should think it luck or god-will that brought us out of there alive."

He heel-turned and walked. Red took a few steps after him, stopped, motioned for Dhorena to follow, and moved on again. It took her shaky breaths and burnsome beats, but she stood and followed after. They walked then as they had walked before—but lighter of flesh and heavier of heart.

The Wilderlands at least were a mite nicer to wander after wading through white and mist. Death walks through the world to grant the black-sleep of nothing, while Mist turns the waking eye to only white. Mist is god in his realm, but Death lives in a world of many gods. If you ask me, children, it is better to suffer a cracked-confederacy of cruel gods than the unbridled tyranny of one. That's just this teller's take.

It was a relief to hear the chatter of beast, bird, and bug—to slog through mud and bramble—to breathe air. The three travelers didn't talk, they weren't happy, but it was some warmth to have the Wilderlands breathing and laughing about them as it should.

They walked in peace with Knalc at the head until he stopped and held up his arm to signal them. All halted.

Quick and quiet, Knalc spider-scurried to an iron oak nearby. Raising two fingers, he reached for the spot he'd seen.

There was a bite taken out of that tree.

Now if you know anything about iron oaks, you know nothing fells them. Not steel or fire or god-smite. Only the hero Hlenniak managed to: using her song, she charmed the king of iron oaks to grant her a branch from which she weapon-weaved a blade to cut, throat to scrote, the seven demon-dimmed warriors who slew her lover, Niakha. But outside of her—and Grand King Iron Oak himself—there ain't Wilderfolk, god, Wastefolk, or Valforian who could so much as scratch an iron oak.

Though there is one sort, a clanless creature, that might concoct such a means.

Knalc took a long sniff of the bite and spat. "Wizards. We need to turn back."

"Wizards?" Dhorena said.

"What makes you think so?" Red asked.

"The smell of magic." Knalc ran his finger against the splinter wood—silk-smooth, iron-hard, and hot. "Feels like wizard work to me. Wizards leave small, impossible things as warnings. They know Wilderfolk will spot them."

Red shook his head. "It's impressive, I'll grant that. But there's no such thing as wizards."

The girl fixed her mind. "What's a wizard?"

"Fantasy," Red laughed. "Pure and simple."

"Spoken like a prim Valforian who don't know shit about tree and root."

Red's smile wilted some. "Whatever it is you just said, it was utterly uncalled for."

"Wizards," Knalc cleared, "are magic-folk. They know how to crack iron wood and carry staves that kill you just by pointing."

"A myth," Red re-countered.

Knalc laughed and motioned him to eye the gash in the tree. "Myth can't crack iron wood."

Here's a tidbit worth knowing—Valforians don't believe in magic. Oh, they have their tricksome steel, their walls, their three gods, but magic ain't a thing they put stock in. Nor should you stock magic—sour stuff as it is. But fools is what I call 'em who put stock in gods but can't fathom flesh warping world with not but will. You ask me, I think they didn't ponder magic none because that would mean they had something to fear. They'd churned up Grandma Dirt, bridged Mist, and beat back Green; they'd made the gods bend to them, but if they thought for a flicker man could wield magic, then they'd have something in this world to fear.

I say that so you can understand Dhorena didn't know a spit of magic.

All she knew of magic came from nightmares and teasing children.

One teasing tale said that the stones in her precious wall were magic and always watching. Now, I know them walls are thick and strong and brazen oft—but they still break or crumble here and there. Well, Dhorena had it whispered to her when she was young, that a soul who didn't mind their parents would end up wall-bound. That while such a soul slept, those stones would get to singing—or moaning more like—to them that don't want to mind their place 'hind the walls. So the wall makes a place for them. The stones sift and shift to make room for a body. Sleeping tight as ever-root, they don't realize they're walking to a new stone-bed.

They get nestled up among their new brothers and, come dawn, that sleepy soul is stone as stone. Only sign it even happened is there's a stone where a stone didn't used to be and empty air in the place a person breathed.

Of all the laugh-lore they churn out, I reason that one is most like to be true. Since the stones they used to build the walls of Illmiv are pulled from below Mount Hush-bee and are splintered souls themselves.

Anyway, I'm telling you all this so you understand why she ran.

She ran because she imagined magic could do anything, and anything was better than what she'd endured to then.

She ran to the wizard because—'fraid though she was—she'd still ready-faced that fear to pull mother and brother back to her. To mend the fraying fabric of her life before the little she still held came unsewn in her grip.

She rampaged through the Wilderlands like a blaze, hardly even fearin' the Green because she knew she'd burn up anything in her path. And the Wilderlands didn't try to stop her. Wizards have their way with the Wilderlands—if they want to be found, they can make it so bark and bush turn a trail to them. No true god-might, but nothing to pick your nose at. If you ever encounter a wizard, don't bother praying; even gods that might bother to help you don't want to get tangled with no wizard. True, a wizard couldn't slay a god, but they might be able to give a lesser god a bruise worth hollering about—and gods won't bother being bruised for the sake of no mortal.

Dhorena didn't know that. She thought she had her Aprheus with her. There were three counts he couldn't help her on: first, gods from outside the Wilderlands don't like walking 'neath branch and over root much—even Wastefolk goddesses fear what might happen if they walked such. Second, she hadn't been keeping no pious mind on her, she'd thought of murder and all but killed Knalc, she'd not kept her brother, she'd not named her kin; the girl was sin riddled. The last you know: Aprheus ain't real.

She knew Knalc and Red were after her and she knew she shouldn't be able to outpace them splint-legged. But somehow, she did. Most like wizard's work—opening up Wilder-way for her but turning it overgrown for Knalc and Red.

She ran the day away, and a good mite of the night. All the while, she didn't catch sight nor sound of the men chasing after her. The wizard didn't care for her to.

The Wilderlands watched and laughed and waited all the while.

And then she stumbled on it.

Though night was fresh-fallen, wizard magic made it seem clear as day. There was a hut made of stone and wood—but not Valforian made. No, this wood was worked on past what Valforians can do and the stones were all sorcersome cut—utterly identical.

There was one entrance with one door heavy enough to ward off the fist of Death should he come knocking, and even then, Death would have to first conquer the iron that had been risen in twisted fashion from the earth. But even should Death conquer the mage-iron and the death-warded door, he would still need to tangle with the wizard.

Dhorena didn't spot the wizard at first. This one watched above it all, perched birdlike at the top of a tree with no branches or leaves, no shade, and no fruit. Green and brown and black, it was hard to tell if it was robes or all just colored flesh-flaps and feathers.

"Wizard!" Dhorena shouted as her heart throbbed and thundered through her chest.

The wizard's staff was pointed at her. She didn't know the rod could end her with a breath, but her very soul warned her once it was level to her. I give her credit though, she didn't flinch—the wizard waited for her to finish speaking and she obliged.

"Wizard!" She started again. "I need your help! My mother, my brother—both have been taken from me by the Wilderlands. I know you have magic, I know you have power over life and death! Anything you ask for that I can provide to you will be yours. Help me or teach me or task me such that I might be reunited with them!"

That really kicked up laughter from the Wilderlands. But she stood, unshook.

The wizard regarded her, then—realizing she had done her yammering—fell ground-ward. Cloth, or leaves, or wings flapped in falling. The drop would have killed you or me, but the wizard landed easy-like and sauntered toward Dhorena.

The closer that wizard came, the more she began to see true. She gasped.

Moss-flesh and beetle-eyed, the wizard seemed hardly human—yet was hunched-up and carried an iron staff in hands that could have been human were it not for their hair. People sing of all the frightsome things wizards do, but some will send you quaking just to behold.

Sure as sin, Blaez Xliv was the sight-quaking sort.

The wizard saw and sniffed and prodded the girl, circling her. The girl looked back. She shook, she quaked, she shuddered, but still she beheld that visage without turning tail.

Then, with whispered incantation, the wizard hefted a leather flask to her from nowhere. The wizard beckoned her to drink from it.

She did.

It was cold and tasteless slipping down, but hitting her stomach it caught flame. She wasn't sure if she was meant to, but she drank it all, feeling the fire in her gut.

The wizard watched.

Stomach churnin' she watched the wizard back.

"What … what was that?"

The thunder of wings and a creaking caw came from overhead and, like a little wizard, a bird—black and braying—landed familiar-like on the wizard's shoulder.

"Necessary," that crow croaked at her. "It was necessary."

A crow talking is a grass blade oddity next to the willow weird wallowing in the Wilderlands. Even from 'hind her wall, Dhorena had heard stories of crows that pecked at the bodies of the dead and learned to speak in their voices. Sometimes widows in Valforian cities would hear a knock and the voice of their lost loves at the door, and—hearts heavy and hopeful—open the door to find the crow that beak-bit the carrion of their mate using their voice in mock-mimic.

Some say the birds must also devour memories of the dead for them to find the homes of their voice-hosts. I reckon that could be true. But I've seen enough to estimate those creatures have enough brains or soul or something else they can muster that much mischief themselves.

Still, in what stories and weavings she had heard, Dhorena did not know of any crow speaking the way this one did. Talkin' for a living being.

The wizard seemed to notice this.

"Mind not my mouth," the crow cawed. "I fed him my own flesh and he now knows my mind."

Dhorena looked from wizard to bird. "Am I speaking to the wizard or the crow?"

The wizard turned a finger face-ward and the crow spoke. "I am the wizard, Blaez Xliv."

Then the finger turned to the bird and, again, the crow spoke. "The bird is Eye. At times I go without him, but Eye does not go without me."

Dhorena wasn't quite sure what to do then. A fearful part of her told her a bow or a curtsey would be the way to go, but she'd never been the bending sort. So she remained standing, her gaze shifting between the pitch black eyes of the wizard and the blacker still bird's beads.

"Great wizard Blaez, I lost my brother to the mist below the bridge, can you bring him back to me?"

"Nay," gurgled the crow.

The raw word burned against her ears so singeingly she nearly wept.

She swallowed and asked, "I lost my mother to the blade of a Wildman. Can you bring her back to me?"

"Nay," Eye said again.

Dhorena couldn't swallow back her tears this time and they dripped past her lips as she shook and said, "Can you do nothing for me?"

For a moment, the wizard and the bird looked at each other. They chirped and cooed and crunched to each other in some low-language. When their congress concluded, the crow flapped over to Dhorena.

She nearly screamed. Wings spread and in flight, she saw the final sight of many a mighty mole or proud possum. Eye landed on her shoulder and even through her clothes, she felt his claws digging into her flesh for the sake of safe perching.

Still twitching and shifting to find comfort on her shoulder, the bird spoke in her ear, breath hot and voice gnarled. "I cannot bring back your brother. I cannot bring back your mother. But there are ways you could commune with them."

She wasn't sure if she asked "how?" but the bird burbled on as if she had.

"When you were shouting and showing and asking and

promising with the niceties of nobility, you said," and here, through some magic that did not require the sacrifice of her flesh, the crow spoke to her in her own voice: "Anything you ask for that I can provide to you will be yours. Help me or teach me or task me such that I might be reunited with them!"

If you've ever heard your own voice breathed perfect-like in your own ear, you know what it is to feel—if only for a second—as though your soul has been sucked from your skin.

"That is what you said," the bird breathed, back in Blaez's tongue. "For my gift, then, there is one thing I must teach you, one thing I must task you, and one thing you will trade me. Then you will know your mother and brother again."

The crow shifted away from her ear to perch on one foot and held out a claw to her in a mockery of the handshakes Valforians prize so highly. "Are we agreed?"

There are few promises more potent than those that are wizard woven. There are few deals darker than those between hand and claw.

Doubt never doused even a corner of Dhorena's determination as she dealt and promised in kind.

XVII

WHAT THE WIZARD TAUGHT DHORENA was how to turn intangible and unspottable by the eyes of beast and bastard.

No, no, I won't tell you how that magic was whipped up. It was easier than you'd think, but danger-dense enough that I don't want any of you spell-stumbling over it. 'Sides, if you happened to work it right, I don't much trust what half of you would get up to.

The wizard tasked Dhorena to scurry her way to Illmiv and rut around in one of the weaker wheres of the wall until loose stones were let free and an entrance of the stomach crawling kind was made.

"Illmiv is not far by mortal miles," the crow mouth of the wizard creaked. "I will bend and knot the woods for you to arrive double fast. Make this entrance and come back here and we will trade."

"What is it that we'll be trading?"

The wizard made a sound that might have been a laugh; the crow craned its head. "That we will discuss once you have returned."

"I'd like to know now, please."

Feathers on the crow and wizard rose. "The deal is made and my promise was of reunion, not information." The feathers settled some. "But this I say for nothing: that which you trade me today, you will not miss tomorrow when you are remingled with your kin."

"And once I have pulled stones from the wall, and made the entrance, what will you use it for?"

The crow spread its wings and let loose a savage screech that'd send you running out of your own skin. "Reunion! Not information!"

Stubborn though that girl was, she shut her mouth and sewed it closed for good measure, smothering her voice while her suspicion surged.

Presently the crow and the wizard calmed. "I will send Eye to watch over you. To make sure you complete your task and my magic works as it ought."

She kept her tongue knotted and nodded her head.

"Then go." The wizard pointed a hand toward the winding Wilderlands and Dhorena turned and walked. As she did, she heard the harpy hum of Eye's wings behind and above her.

As she went her way in the Wilderlands, she knew bug and bird, man and monster, possum and pine all caught no scent or sight or taste or trace of her as she moved. Yet that crow she could feel eyeing her back even through the magic Blaez had taught her.

Just as the wizard had worded, the Wilderlands seemed to warp themselves around her as she went. Each step felt like a hundred as miles shrank under her feet and a journey of days turned tiny.

Before she could quite say how it happened, she found herself toe-to-stone with the wall of Illmiv.

Oh, children, chilly as you are now—bundled and battling winter's weight—I tell ya, you can't imagine a colder reunion.

There that girl was, at the very wall she'd been battling toward, but she knew that—with no mother, no brother, no father—there wasn't much she hankered for beyond that stone other than the feeling of her own bed.

So, with that crow still tailing her, she started to circle that endless wall.

She knew those stones near as well as any of you might know the trees and trails around here. She'd walked the other side of them a hundred-hundred times. Though it was her first time seeing them close-like from Wilder-side, she knew when she passed by the empty bakery, or the jewel store her mother'd always loved, or the shabby antique store she hadn't entered since losing her father—the frivolous fineries of those self-styled civil folk.

All the while, soldiers in armor clattered and blathered at the top of that wall, watching for the sort of sight that was right under their noses: the Wilderlands creeping into their city. The wizard's word proved true enough in that they didn't even have a god-sent notion that Dhorena might be there.

Now, that wall was mightsome enough to never break, an army couldn't carve the thing apart. The girl's parents had held high seats behind that wall, and knew where was weaker and what might crumble first if the gorish gods gobsmacked all four side with full force. But more helpful was that Dhorena had been a child ahind those walls, and children go places they shouldn't and know the small wonders of big things.

There was a spot any Valfling her age knew held loose stones.

To be sure, once those kids came of wiser age and had their own high seats 'hind those walls, they'd spruce up those stones. But to the cackling kids 'hind those walls with only three gods to mind, loose stones in a wall were a potent profanity, a sense of strange power worth keeping secret.

Like she knew the antique shop and the jeweler and the bakery, Dhorena knew when she had come to where the stones on the inside were loose.

From the outside there wasn't no notion that this part of the wall was any more weary than the rest, but she knew this was where to make her wound. She drew Red's sword and set to slow, sorry work—carving away at the space between stones with Valforian steel.

Even as naked day turned to blushing eve and shame-black night, she was not seen.

Now, even as her work turned her fingers raw under the gaze of Eye, Dhorena wasn't no fool. She didn't have any aim to let a wizard wander leisure-like into Illmiv, deal or none. So, as she pried and levered and pulled brick and stone loose, she made sure the way she made was only a size smidge more than big enough for her.

All tellers agree she spent two nights on this task. True or tall, two's what all tellers tout. When the sun rose on the third day, her hands were toil tattered, her eyes and stomach churned, and her knees throbbed like bursting crocus bulbs. But Red's Valforian steel remained untarnished and her work was done.

She turned her back on that hard hewn home hole she'd made and—though she'd made it with minor mischief—the crow didn't seem to mind none as she started to walk back toward Blaez, trusting the Wilderlands would be wizard warped again.

Easy as sin, she found the way back to Blaez. But Dhorena still had a hair-standing feeling about that wizard and the task given. Halfway through her walking back, she leaned with half-feigned fatigued against a hearty stone.

She hadn't given Red or Knalc a thought since she'd found the wizard, but if Blaez turned traitor on her, she didn't want to risk them not knowing. Even exhausted as she was, that girl was vengeance vested. So, with a finger already bloodied from her wall-work, she drew a mark Knalc was like to know and Red was certain to.

Eye watched, chittering to himself.

In a matter of breaths she was on her feet and pushing forward again.

When she found the wizard waiting—cheating her chatter of her chicanery—she told of what she'd done at the wall.

Once her telling was through, the wizard looked to Eye. The bird swooped back to the wizard and the two chittered in their private tongue again.

Finally, Eye looked back to Dhorena. "As you say, so it has been done."

"Good," said Dhorena. "Now what is it you want me to trade to you?"

I tell ya, if birds could smile.

"You are high-born Valforian, are you not?" Eye asked.

"I am," the girl answered.

"And your family, they shared secrets with you did they not? Novelties only told to those of noble blood?"

"… I suppose so."

If crows' mouths could water, the world would have drowned then-there.

"Secrets of the things long buried beneath the Sword Tower. Secrets of the world before it was fire burned and green swallowed. Secrets known only to rocks and rotting folk and the rare handful bequeathed that inheritance."

She said nothing, for no question was asked.

She said nothing because, while she had heard the odd rumor or the strange fact she shouldn't have, her parents never whispered to her about secluded secrets of dead years. Usually they'd read her small children's tales, things to help little ones sleep.

Dhorena didn't much think Blaez was fixed on fables, but more ferocious things.

"What I want," the crow raved on with ravenous eyes, "is the most earth spoiling secret in your skull."

First she lied. "If you have a question, I'll happily tell you the answer." Then she told the truth. "I don't think I know the worst secret I know."

Eye took flight, circling Dhorena. "You don't have to think a thing to know it. I can dig and draw it out of you. When I'm done, you won't even mind what I've mined."

"I won't remember whatever secret you take?"

"Sounds like you don't much remember it now, eh?"

"But—but after that … you'll reunite me with my brother and mother?"

"As I said, so it shall be."

The wizard motioned for her to follow deeper into the unnatural abode.

A thousand voices told her "no" and "don't" and "run" and "stop" and "kill" and fearful idlings of every ilk. Yet in the center of that swirl of fight and flight was a single, terrible solace: "maybe."

Maybe the wizard will hold true to promise. Maybe I will see my mother and brother again. Maybe, maybe, maybe, maybe everything can be all right.

Ain't a one of you can tell me you haven't had a day where a "maybe" was all you needed in your ear to be willing to stake your own soul.

So—with a "maybe" in her mind—she walked behind Blaez, deep into that den which even Death feared to enter.

"WE SHOULD HAVE FOUND HER by now." That was less than the sum of it. The two men had been looking for seven suns and hadn't found proof or print of the girl's fleeing. "How good a tracker are you really?" Red wondered.

Knalc had gone to doubling back and turning over leaves to spot any lost footprint, but couldn't find nothing. He wasn't a tracker by trade—but any Wilderfolk who can chew their meat can find evidence of a Valfling's ramble bluster through the Wilderlands.

"Can't find what the Wilderlands is hiding from me," Knalc spat.

They'd spent the first days looking only for Dhorena but ran dry on food in quick time. They then took to hunting and scavenging to keep themselves alive as they linger-looked.

They found some squirrels and hares and woodwarblers to snack on and the pair hauled some water from a southern stream where they nearly nicked a ram-cow that skedaddled as soon as it sniffed them out—those beasts is impossible to fall without arrow and bow.

All-done, they got enough to get 'em by, and in getting by they turned back to tracking the girl. They had a mite less luck in that.

"What do you want to do if we can't find her?"

"Nothing," Red said. "I failed her mother. I failed her brother. If she is dead, then I will have fully failed in my duty. We find her, or nothing."

Knalc nodded. "What if we do find her? What if we find a body?"

Red stopped in his tracks. His hand went to the knife—the mother's knife—'round his belt. He didn't draw or brandish it, just nudged Knalc's noggin to the truth that it was there. "Are you keeping anything from me, Wildman?"

Knalc smiled. *"Less than you think. But more than you'd like."*

Red just waited.

"No," Knalc said. "Not keeping anything. If I knew or thought the girl dead, I'd tell you. She's gone. Simple as sin."

Red sighed. "Then we keep looking until we find something."

Without else to do, they did—but they were finding more bruises and bug bites than worthful stuff. They were losing blood and time and they'd already lost a lot of both when they'd started. Red and Knalc searched past the setting of the sun—letting sky and earth go cold around them.

Mamma Moon was full-faced that night, pale and imperfect— Knalc looked up at her as they stopped to eat by the light of moon and stars.

Knalc didn't much care for recalling tales, but sitting in moonlight eating in silence with a man he had—and might yet—aim to kill, made him go soft and somber-headed.

"What do Valforians say about the Moon?"

Red ripped into some rabbit meat and chewed long afore answering. "Moon's the moon."

"I know the Moon's the fucking Moon. Any stories about it?"

Again, Red ripped into his meat and thought some on it. "They say the moon was made by men long ago. Long before the

Wilderlands rampaged over the earth. Men made the moon to get away from the Wilderlands—they threw it up into the heavens and Aprheus, in his wisdom, didn't strike it down. So then men flung themselves up there once the Wilderlands started getting overgrown, to escape. Those that are up there are Aprheus's chosen few. All of us down here on earth are left to prove ourselves of worth to Him, or else be gobbled by the Goat-Below. All of those who got away from the end of the world get to live and die and know their souls are safe. We have trials here to test us. Trials that happen all through our lives. The more trials we pass and the more good we do, the lighter our souls become, making it easier for Pearlaphine to fling them to salvation.

"If our souls are light enough, they reach the realm of Aprheus. But if our souls are heavy, mired by sin and wretchedness, Pearlaphine flings them only to watch them drop like a rock to the Goat-Below; the heavier the soul, the more it fills his belly and the stronger he becomes. One day he'll gobble so much he'll be able to break free and march on the moon. When that day comes, we've got to pray there have been more strength of number in good souls than wicked ones. The Goat-Below will either be thrown back down, or he'll gobble all our souls and sit, bloated, upon the throne of the earth."

Knalc drank in these words long and silent, then he spat. "Shit story."

Red got a bit rustled by that. "What?"

"You heard. *Shit story.*"

He huffed. "Yeah? And how do you figure that?"

"How you throw yourself?"

"Pardon?"

"You said men threw themselves up there." Knalc held up his arms—calloused, swollen, scarred, muscular. "I couldn't throw anything that far, so how'd they throw themselves up there to the Moon?"

"Probably with a catapult of some sort."

"*You're making words up!* I don't know what a catapult is, but what I do know is I couldn't throw myself no matter how hard I tried."

Red sighed. "They had … more back then than we do now."

Knalc wasn't having none of it. "Sure, sure. But how did they throw that far? Even if they threw really well, they'd have to throw a mite better than me. And I'm mean at throwing."

"Fine," Red chewed on his final meal scraps. "What do Wilderfolk think of the moon then?"

"First," Knalc said, "we know the Moon ain't a place. Moon is a goddess, one of the oldest. That's how she pulls wind and water. That's how she has that *silver luster.*"

"There's only three gods, Wildman," Red scoffed. "All that is only has power because they will it so."

"So the gods took your name from you? Seems to me you'd hate those gods."

"No," Red growled. "Men took my name from me … I took my name from me because of what I've done."

"It's your gods either way," Knalc prodded. "Your gods gave you power and gave power to those who stripped your name away. I wouldn't love no god like that."

"It's the same for Wilder-gods," Red sneered. "You think Moon cares more about you than Aprheus cares about his children?"

"Wilder-gods never give *shit*," Knalc said. "They only take. Grandma Dirt takes our bodies, Death bottles-up our breath, and all the other gods smash our souls for sport below Mount Hush-bee. I am what I am. No god had hand in molding me."

Red muttered almost like he didn't want Knalc to hear, but there wasn't no one else to note the hissed curse: "Heathen."

"The only gods that don't take is Pappa Sun and Mamma Moon," Knalc butted back. He looked up at that sky—star strewn and wild but for Mamma Moon keeping all those lights in line, keeping bears and boars and belts as they should be in the sky. Knalc knew without her, the stars would bounce and twist and burn each other. "Those two are the only gods worth more than liking."

I'll weave you the story Knalc whispered to Red—for when he spoke it, it was in Valforian and stories in Valforian don't sing like Wildertongue, even the lowest of our tellers could word-whip the tallest Valforian-teller. You all have already heard this tale as far back as when all you minded were teat and tears, but maybe you ain't heard me weave it for you.

Back afore Time had taken flight, afore sun or moon shifted through the sky, there was just Grandma Dirt, and she would look up at the great above and, for whatever flew by before time came to be, she was lonesome. Not mate-hankering or loin-hungry, but she wanted another, someone she could see and know as she looked about. So she sunder-yanked her own flesh and flung it skyward— that became Mamma Moon. And Grandma Dirt liked her daughter and smiled to see her hanging high above and looking back at her.

Mamma Moon set to work, making the wings of Time and all other things that soar through sky, she filled the curves of her mother to keep her flesh good for food and forests. She pulled up mounds of earth in other places so she could reach out and touch her mother as she passed through the sky.

But time makes all good things go to rot.

Mamma Moon got to feeling lonely too and hers was a deeper longing than her mother's. This was a loin-hunger, a mate-hankering. Moon didn't have means to make a mate of her own, but she knew how it was done 'cause Grandma Dirt shared all her secrets with her daughter.

So, while Grandma Dirt was slumbering, Mamma Moon crept

toward the horizon and dipped into her mother, finding that molten red that thunders through her like blood. She seized it and crafted it careful-like and placed it in the sky and made Pappa Sun.

And Pappa Sun lit the dark places of the world and set Green about the earth and smiled rainbows into the sky. And when Grandma Dirt woke, she didn't mind none, her daughter was happy. And Sun and Moon together made mortal man to walk the earth and celebrate their union.

While Mamma Moon had been wrapped in her mate-hankering, she hadn't noticed that Time had gotten to its own makings. Death came into this world—made to do as Time would want. The only task Death was saddled with was taking, harvesting, reaping, ripping. Death didn't think high or low of this job, took no joy in seizing and stealing—the duty was fixed and Death saw it done. Not wrathful or gleeful or hatesome, Death is dutiful.

But Pappa Sun and Mamma Moon, in their jubilation, made it impossible for Death's work to be done. Together they bliss-drowned the earth so everything had means to live forever, and without the food of souls, Death began to wither. What would you do if the lacking of work—work that brought you neither joy nor hate—began to unwind you?

So Death, desperate and hungry, pulled Pappa Sun from the sky while he was sleeping and hid him 'hind the mountains. When Mamma Moon came back from tending the sea and tides, she was shook to see Death—normally cold and calm—in a frenzy.

"It was Mist!" Death rattled. "Mist rose up and swallowed Sun and made off with him!" And he pointed Mamma Moon over the horizon opposite of where he'd hidden Sun. "Quick! Quick! Fast now! Heave-run and you might just catch them!"

Mamma Moon didn't think to question Death. Death—until now—had never bothered to lip-lie. She took off after her love and never bothered to look over her shoulder to see Death sneak back toward the horizon.

Once there, Death shook Pappa Sun awake. Pappa Sun didn't have time to puzzle out why he'd woke in a strange place 'cause he was stun-shocked at Death dancing up and down and shouting so.

"Run! Run! Fastlike now!" Death cawed. "It was Unglog! He got hungry and he snatched up Moon and now he's running off with her, slobbersome, with plans to swallow her whole!" And Death—knowing that Sun was just thread-shy of Moon sprinting—pointed to the same horizon he'd sent Moon over. "That way! They went that way! If you take off now, you might just catch Unglog before Moon rounds his stomach."

Pappa Sun didn't waste a breath. Leaving a trail of flames and sizzling air across the sky, he took off in the direction Death had pointed him.

Soon as he was fled, Death found Time and asked this: "Make it so Moon and Sun are caught in this beat-breath. Make it so that they are forever tailing each other 'cross the sky and heavens. Then I will better be able to do your work. Together they give so much that Time means nothing—folks don't heed what they don't fear and Death cannot stand against them. But separate and mind-set on tracking down the other, they won't have mind or means of keepin' humans safe. I—Death—can go about my work again and people will fear and heed you."

And so Time did this. He bound up all his power in makin' sure Moon and Sun shifted through the sky. Time cursed 'em to run the same trail 'cross the heavens until they burn through both.

Cry and weep whenever you watch the Sun set while the Moon peeks over the horizon—for that is Moon catching tail of her lover only to have him vanish. It's same-like at sunrise when Sun gets a look-see at his lost lover.

But there was a crack in old Death's plan.

Sun was that thread-width slower than Moon, and Grandma

Dirt built her body and the heavens 'round it like an apple. Lick an apple in one direction and you trail back to where you started. Moon was able to catch Sun!

Rejoice and sing when Moon and Sun are heaven met—for that is the union of two lost loves! Majestic and summer-bright are both those heavenly bodies, but so enraptured by their union are they that they focus all their god-might on loving the other. They both go night-black in their passion to better know the other.

Miracles bubble 'bout in that time, children. Under a moon-shadow sky are many a union brought to be; and those conceived while all is dark are god-touched.

But they are time cursed. In the beats it'd take a pair to undo belt and breaches, the black is already starting to fade. Sun and Moon are forced apart and, until Death is conquered, our mortal sort will never know their share-glory.

And that is where Knalc finished the tale.

"Shit story," Red said—though he brushed salt from his eye.

Knalc stared with narrow eyes at the moon. Stared at it until his eyes were glow-stung and salty too. He shook away and smiled a dead man's grin. "Yeah," he said. "It's still a shit story."

Red nodded and ran rattling fingers over the place an arm had once been. He clutched at the cloth that covered it—angersome.

Long was the buzz and wail of the Wilderlands and long was the night-sigh as it blustered against them—but neither man were bent to blanket or bed. Long are the lives of those who know the dead and dying.

Red's fingers relaxed, and he stopped his phantom-clutching. "I don't believe I've asked you your name."

"No," the other nodded. "You haven't."

And he never did. There they sat: one man, red and nameless, and the other having name he never spoke.

The long night wound on.

 **XIX**

WINTER WAS COMING IN LIKE a fresh tooth when they finally found hint of her.

Though never chumsome or kin-like, Knalc and Red never ceased their nosing about. The Wilderlands had been kind to them—kind in that it hadn't been cruel. It was Red who managed to catch that first whiff of Dhorena. You might go thinkin' Red was able to spot it 'cause he'd finally started to get some Wilder-wits about him. Nay, he spotted it 'cause it was a mark he knew better than any name he'd had.

It was a grey stone they'd never wandered upon before or hence—blood-varnished on it was a pronged lightning bolt.

"She was here," Red said. His single hand took to shivering as he rubbed the rock, like this blood-made lightning was rattling his joints.

"You don't know that," Knalc said, knowing he knew the mark but not from where. "There are Wilder and Wastefolk who might have left that mark."

"No," Red said. "She's the only one who'd draw this mark out here."

"You sure?"

"Sure as sin." He didn't know what the words were, but he'd

heard Knalc say 'em enough that he had a taste for their meaning.

Wizards ain't got need of paths or trails for hunting and travel—they just bend the Wilderlands to their will when they travel. Way I hear it, some wizards don't even need to walk or wade to reach a place, with naught but words and will they can whisper themselves 'hind any tree or rock. Point being, there was no way to true-tell where the wizard's lair was—they weren't much better off than the wandering they'd been at afore, 'cept now they knew they were close.

So they walked beyond the stone, in a direction they were a hair more than half sure they'd never wandered afore. The Wilderlands seemed to be chanting around them.

Woodwarblers wailed against bark and branch like war drums. Crows cawed in careful rhythm as they circled high above. Wrens rang out a tune of mourning as the travelers went on their way. The trees themselves hummed a croaking tune of doom and death. A single laughing-cat, far away, stung a note above it all; it was hard to know the cut of that laugh 'cause all laughing-cat sounds seem as mockery.

But they were not hindered. No silver tips, no night-swoops, and the laughing-cat stayed his distance. They were allowed to go on their way—hard to say if this was wizard-will, Green taking pity on their plight, or Grandma Dirt knowing what's best. But Knalc and Red didn't care. Unimpeded, they passed into the wizard-growth.

They saw what Dhorena had moons back—a hut that wasn't a hut, lit by light that couldn't be, and a twisted wall of iron that seemed to have been summoned from the earth to protect whatever was behind it. The wizard was outside, cross-legged, staff on lap, and waiting.

The Wilderlands beat and sang and cawed and laughed louder around them as they drew closer.

Knalc's voice was scarce louder than a breath. "Said there was such a thing as wizards, didn't I?"

"A person in the woods, sitting," Red said, self-blind to the miracles wrought around him. "I can only dread what magic might follow such a terrible thing."

They stopped several sword lengths from the wizard.

When the wizard didn't mind or note them none, Knalc spoke.

"You understand Wilder-speak?" Knalc asked.

The wizard beheld Knalc and nodded.

Afore Knalc could speak again, one of the crows in the murder-circle above fell on them like night, landing on a branch just above Red and Knalc.

"I do, Eye does," said the crow. "But I understand Valforian tongue better."

Both men set their hands to the blades at their side at the soul-sound coming from that crow.

Their startling made the wizard wheeze, humorsome.

Under those soot-shot, skim-smooth eyes there were teeth more akin to a skull's than a living being's, and through those time-tested teeth the wizard cackled. Yes, that laugh was cough-clouded, but it was still clear that brainrot had seeded itself in the wizard. Knalc noted this, but Red hadn't witnessed brainrot afore.

"So," said the crow for the wizard. "Why are you at my door?"

"We can be a bit more civil than that," Red said, heart still hammering, looking from crow to caster. "Whom do we have the honor of meeting?"

"Blaez Xliv."

Red leaned toward Blaez in not quite a bow. "My friend thinks you're a wizard."

"Do you not?"

"I had my ... misgivings," Red glanced again at the crow. "Is it true?"

The wizard laughed and the warbler spoke. "Why wouldn't it be? Now answer me, what brings you to my door?"

"Searching for a girl," Knalc said. "We've looked since before winter. Have you spotted anyone?"

The smile slid from the wizard's lips. Fingers toyed some with the staff—looking away from Knalc and Red.

"What makes you think she's here?"

"Her family crest," Red said. "Painted in blood on a stone not two miles yon."

The wizard mumbled some gib-speak afore rising to feet, staff held loose in hand. "Blood spots many stones in the Wilderlands."

"Yes," Red said, marking that metal-rod in case it took to marking him. "That's why I think if I see a specific crest in blood, it means I'm near the thing I'm looking for."

"We're all searching for something."

Caresome to not go threatening those who claimed to be wizards, Red rested his thumbs through his belt to show the knife—the Valforian steel Dhorena's mother once carried with that same symbol held on its pommel. "You still haven't answered our question. Have you seen anyone come through here?"

"What do you want with her?"

"Our want isn't your worry," Red said. "I take it you've seen her?"

Fingers thrummed against the steel of the staff. Feathers ruffled. "I can take you to her. So long as you are willing to trade."

Red shook his head. "I'm looking for the girl. I'm not here to make bargains."

The crow took flight.

The attack didn't come from the staff. In honest, it didn't come from the wizard at all, but the wizard was the root of the happening, true as breath.

The staff-less hand whipped under robes or flesh and pulled a wand.

"Shit," Knalc breathed and flung himself to the dirt.

But Red didn't have the measure of wizard-tricks. He didn't think to dodge or duck until the happening had passed.

The wand glowed red. There came a sundering sound.

Hell-heat licked 'em—when Red turned he was smacked to the ground, left to stun-stare next to Knalc.

An elm that must have been as old as Time was wreathed in wrathful red and orange and yellow flame. Ripped down the middle as if lightning-split, smoke and ash bled from the crater-crack and washed over the two men, stinging their eyes and lungs.

Brainrot laughter spilled gleefully from the wizard as the crow landed shoulder-wise. "Mortal men who come to me are here to do what I believe they are here to do. I believe you're here to bargain." A hairy hand pointed to the steel at Red's waist. "You go showing off that steel. It looks mighty good. Give me that knife and I can show—not give—show you the girl."

Horror-racked and fear-wrought, Red did just that—pulling knife from belt he threw it to the wizard's feet.

The bird swooped to it and snatched the weapon for the wizard. Blaez let off some tiny laughs and then hid it away in a fold of flesh or robes. Standing, Blaez Xliv moved toward the hut that wasn't a hut and motioned for the two men to follow.

I want you to remember children—you always have a choice in things. But that don't matter, 'cause you bein' who you are can only ever make one choice at any given time-place. As long as you be you, you really don't got much choice at all. So Knalc and Red— being Knalc and Red—did the only thing they could do being who they were: they followed after.

Behind them—the elm still roared with fire and pain and time, forgotten to the pyre of the ages.

I tell you, for the first time in breathing memory, the Wilderlands had gone silent and all through them there was only that fire roaring.

They followed Blaez Xliv to the iron-made wall while the wizard wrestled with some ingredients and utterings, back turned to Knalc and Red but with the crow ever watching. There was some rattling as the wizard unraveled the bewitchment. The metal gasped and swung open, welcoming them as best as cold things hewn and harvested from the earth can.

Stepping through, they were brought to the hut that wasn't a hut. The light that couldn't have been sun looked down on them as the wizard again unraveled the way forward. Just like the iron before it, the door opened and they went in.

I'm going to try, children. I'm going to try to tell you of this room, but I ain't got words for what I don't know.

That room had light with no roots or way floating over head to brighten a room of flasks made of metal and silver. Some of these flasks were marked by script, others by the faces of the damned. Stray grey vines or rope ran about to bind it all together in pagan harmony. Shelves with paper—bound, folded in animal flesh and unfrayed, if you can believe it. Too much paper to comprehend, piles beyond possibility. And there were windows the like of which you ain't seen afore, showing not the other side of the wall, but a place beyond. All the room hummed with wizard-might. The Wilderland has its hum and wizard lairs have theirs—low and flavorless.

Red reached for one of the windows but Knalc stopped his hand and shook his head. *"Better not."* Knalc himself was fighting a gut-yanking to reach through the windows himself, but he knew that any gut-yank you get while on wizard land is best fought against.

They walked on and Blaez Xliv led them through another door.

This one had no enchantment. Blaez opened it and led them back to where she grew.

There was more smoke than air in that room.

Knalc's feet crunched against leaves and vines. He thought he was under open sky for a breath, but no, it was far too dark. It was certainly a room, just more dirt and grass than floor, more growth and green than wall.

He and Red saw her at the same time.

She was wrapped in weeds and green—shaded to earth-like tones by roots sprung up from below which turned her toes and feet bramble-bound while bulbs popped from flesh and stretched sinew. She'd sprouted a garish green with garner-grown vines of vitriol winding about her waist and neck. Her eyes had taken the peal of poison, her face more fern than flesh. They wouldn't have marked her human had they not seen the sword at her waist, constricted by vines and overgrowth, and had they not known her afore she succumbed to weed and wizard-green.

She didn't seem to know them as they came in. She didn't even seem alive by human measures.

Knalc could hear the roar of blood raging through Red followed in fast form by the roar spat from his tongue. "What the fuck is this! What have you done?"

The wizard laughed and laughed and laughed and laughed and broke to breathe only to laugh and laugh and laugh again.

Red tried to move on the wizard, but Knalc held him back. Red reached for Knalc's sword, but Knalc blocked it from him easy and held the man in place.

Blaez was still chortling as the crow put on a mocksome voice. "'I need your help wizard! My mother, my brother, are both dead. You do magic. I know you bend life and death! Anything! Anything you ask for I'll give. Help me! Teach me! Send me to them!" The wizard spat and walked to her, poking at what would have been her face with the end of his staff. "She's with them now. Though it was a rank trade."

Her face was stiff, she didn't even seem to feel the prodding. Laugher cracked the wizard's lips again.

Over the course of this, Red had gone cold-still. "You killed her then."

"No. She wanted to see the dead and that's what she is doing. She traded her most smothered secret to do so. But it was rotten."

Red went even colder—his eyes blazing at the wizard. "What secret?"

"The girl implied she had secrets of the hidden chambers behind Illmiv's walls," The crow said. "But my green has been hard rooting through her mind and I haven't turned up more than mutterings. The hardest secret to hit in there was that she loves her father, if you can believe it. Worthless. I let her keep it. Seemed to be more of a bruise to her brain than balm. But I don't mind, I have a way through that wall now. And if I am wrong, I can bleed my hex from her and see her promise kept."

Red turned pale.

"Maybe we can make another deal," Knalc said. "Wizards like to make deals don't they?"

Slow-like, the wizard's head went cocked, noggining on the thought for a moment.

"I want the girl."

"You already have the girl,"

"One cannot own themselves," the crow said. "I can't keep her past her promise unless you grant me leave to. That is the way of things."

Red's teeth were grinding. "And what would you do with her?"

The wizard gave a tiny laugh now. The crow's words went so low as to be hard-heard. "My want isn't your worry."

"Cut her down."

"No."

"Cut … her … down."

"Nay."

Red relaxed and Knalc thought he had resigned himself—that they would begin bargaining now.

Not so.

A flare of strength surged through Red. Even with one arm, he somehow wrestled and slipped from Knalc's grasp in seconds. At first, Knalc thought he was running right for Blaez—the wizard thought like and readied staff.

But Red veered away from Blaez as magic burst from the staff. Reality cracked for just a moment, but missed Red, making a scattered hole in the wall through which light seeped in.

Red went for Dhorena—the wizard caught this and swung the staff hard at him. But Red spun away, leaving the staff to wave through only empty air.

He was close enough now to seize his need from Dhorena's side.

Lightning lurched his hand—Red reared for his friend, his death-maker. It ripped through root and vine easy as flesh and vein. He lacked a hand and was time-rusted, but he knew his steel and it knew him. It hummed for him bard-bars that come with blood and battle.

"Cut her free." He didn't speak to the wizard now, but to Knalc—those were the only words he wasted.

Though steel had lessened him, though time had frayed him, though Wilderlands had turned him ragged—Red moved fast and smooth and death-poised as ever. Such a storm of blows sliced and slashed at Blaez that no magic or inhuman-might could Blaez call on while being driven from the room, already blood sopped.

The wizard had no time to remember that, in leading these strangers in, all wards were rendered wide open, meaning Death could walk wherever he willed.

Knalc worked fast to cut Dhorena loose. His mind was made foggy by the smoke and he found it hard telling where green gave way to flesh. If he did slice skin, the girl didn't seem to know or feel or care. She just stared, unblinking and green-yellow.

Red was making the battle hard fought. The wizard was trying to conjure some wicked trick to get a fighting edge on Red who wasn't havin' it. Blaez tried to twist and better aim that staff—but Red would lean in hard and push the rod skyward. Blaez reached for the wand that had struck down the tree—Red batted the wizard's hand away. Blaez dove for cover in the lair and Red stormed right after, not granting Blaez breath or breadth.

The crow soared and cawed frightfully overhead, molting-mad and peppering his bleeding master with feathers as if such could clot the growing culmination of wounds.

They say wizard blood is magic. That you can make poison or poth from it depending on the goal of the hands 'hind the brewing. But the important thing is this: they bleed. Any beast or being that bleeds can be killed and Blaez was bleeding heavy.

The wizard's robe-flesh had gone red with leaking life. Blaez knew a thing more than feathers must be done fast or else Red would bring Death.

Muttering a charm of speed, Blaez rushed past Red. In going, the wizard got a tendon near torn by Red's steel-snickering. Blaez burst from the hut, barely living and hard of breath, Blaez spun to ground, landing gut to dirt. Then, rolling over, took quick aim.

Red was raging right behind, all steel and vengeance, fire and fury and despair.

For a beat, Blaez saw the whole of the Wilderlands reflected in that Valforian steel.

Blaez let loose a blast of magic.

Riiiiiiiiiiiiichhhooow!!!

Reality ripped.

You ever feel the touch of wizard might through your flesh? It's a rancid blow. Like your insides are burning up and fluttering out of you—oft times they're doing one or both. Worst of all, that magic is so quick you can't see it. Once a wizard has hard-locked eyes set on you, ain't no dodging it.

Red was fast. But not that fast.

His left side was blown away in a burst of flesh and bone.

Marrow and malice fell from him. He staggered, clutching his gasping wound.

He had to catch himself with his sword, wielding it like a staff. He seemed to be about to speak—and spat blood instead.

Blaez and him looked at one another, their blood mingled bosom-close in the dirt and feathers.

Then, slow-like, rage swelled and sorrow deepened, and Red's eyes became like a funeral-pyre, mad for more kindling.

Though his guts were on the ground, he stood and walked toward the wizard.

The crow swooped with stabbing talons, but fell to Red's sword like a fly licked off the wind.

The Wilderlands had gotten back to laughing. Death had taken notice, and walked closer now.

It was hard to see the blood covering his coat 'cause of the red.

Blaez backed away, shocked that Red was on his feet at all. He ought to be dead, yet Red walked forward. Blaez started pulling powder and stone from flesh-cloth to prepare more bursts of magic. But shaking hands are hard to do spell work with. Blaez backed-up further still.

The burning elm looked on and Red did not slow.

Blaez dropped powder and stones and they were scattered to the wind. The wizard screamed.

Red smiled a crimson smile. He readied his sword.

It was then that Knalc came out of the hut—carrying Dhorena, neither plant nor person, in his arms. He saw the two and spotted the bird body and the trail of blood leading toward them—and saw the wizard reach for the wand.

"No!" Knalc shouted.

Hard to say just how it happened next.

The wand glowed red.

The man in the red coat must have heard Knalc shout or saw the wand-reach, but he couldn't stop what happened next.

Red went up in smoke and fire.

"… nnnnnnnnnnnooooooooooo …" the mass of skin and bramble that was Dhorena groaned—sounding less like a voice and more like bark creaking or wind moving through leaves.

The wizard let out another laugh. Triumphant and imperious— but Blaez's lips slipped to celebration too soon.

With the might of a god pummeling a soul from Hush-bee Mountain, Red threw his sword right through Blaez's wrenched heart.

The wizard's laugh turned to a bleeding shout and then a cry! And now Red was laughing—though he burned—high and clear above it all. Laughing with the Wilderlands.

With what strength she had, Dhorena rolled out of Knalc's hands and began to claw and root her way toward the burning man.

"… nnnnnnnnnooooooooooo …"

And Death came there at last to find the skewered wizard.

Remember, Death takes no joy in the work assigned. But there was perhaps a smile on ol' Death's face while pruning the soul of that skewered sorcerer.

As Death pulled that final thread off, Blaez's scream withered. Death put the wizard's soul in a sack and then looked to Red. Charred and still whooping in victory, Red was hardly recognizable as a man.

Death, I say, did feel a small hint of almost-sadness. Far from the aching you or I might feel when a person passes, but Death looked at the man and the girl crawling toward him and understood, or understood enough.

Death breathed in, filling lungs that hadn't heaved in ages, and blew hard at Red. The breath of Death extinguished flame and pain. Red sack-crumpled to the ground. Death walked toward him and Red smiled, not 'cause of Death, but because his daughter had reached him.

"… nnnnnnnnnooooooooo …"

He couldn't speak, he'd spent the last of his breath yelling and whooping.

Tears spilled from her eyes, some turned to steam as they pattered against Red, others stuck to him like sap. The green that caked her fingers burned as she ran her hands over him.

"… doooooooonn't … leeeeaaaavve …"

Red smiled at his daughter.

Death waited over him.

"… ppppllleeeeeaaaaasssee …"

Red waited.

Knalc waited.

Death waited.

"… fffaaaatheeeerrr …"

Death leaned forward—

But Red wasn't watching Death. He looked at his flesh, his blood, his daughter, and felt the sting of tears in his eyes. He smiled, not red, but wide and white as winter-root.

And then his soul slipped from him.

Dhorena had named him "Father" for though that was not the name he was born by, it was the only one he'd ached to have pinned to him again. His wanting was sated as he left this world. Most ain't that lucky.

Shock or weariness of body or heart, it's hard to say, but as Red's soul slipped away, Dhorena collapsed.

I want you to know that his soul came off light and easy. I need you to know that the man was a hero whose true name, I'm sad to say, I don't recall. But I'll call him Nicholus from here out when I must.

Work done and bodies collected, Death left that place.

Knalc was all there was left standing.

And as Death left, the bodies of the crow, the wizard, and Red caught fire and were gone in moments. All that remained were the knife and sword. Men burn and die, but Valforian steel outlives us all.

THE KNIFE OF HER MOTHER and the sword of her father hung from her belt. Her brother had had no name and thus had nothing and so she had nothing to remember him by proper-like, just "Amok," a name he had never known. And there was Knalc—lingering on her like a dead limb, still clinging even as the rest of the body turns to deeper rot.

The green-sick she'd had pumpin' through her veins took a long while to bleed away. Two days there'd been no change in her and she drank naught but water and sunlight; after that she'd started breathing again and chewing what food was put to her tongue. Three days later she would blink and moan and speak briefly. Three more days and she managed to sit and speak and think the way she should. One day after that, she buried the ashes of her father.

They walked as far from the wizard's lair as their legs would let 'em tread. They didn't quite break free from the Wilderlands, but they were able to see Hush-bee Mountain and the four-faced god on the far horizon.

It was Dhorena who did it all. Even though her bones and muscles were still worn from wretched wizard work, she dug the grave, she lowered in the bag his ashes were gathered in, she filled the hole, she found a slab of stone, and spent the time etching

Valforian speak onto it—"Nicholus of Illmiv: Husband, Father, Hero"—she then took the time to go out and collect what flowers she could fathom: bloomshade, red-yarrows, and maydays mingled on his makeshift grave.

Once they were placed, she spoke a prayer over them. Now, I don't know the words to no heretic prayers and it was clear neither did she, not in full—but I think if her gods were real they would have been moved all the same. Say a prayer for her tonight if you think of it and then whisper another for Red.

When finished, she knelt there, looking at the grave—not enough water in her body to bring tears to her eyes.

Knalc watched her all while he started a campfire far enough away so as not to disrupt her suffering, but close enough that it might grant her some small warmth as she mourned. At the sun's rising he would hunt and gather what he could and come back to find her still there.

She stayed kneeling there for two nights.

Three dead and only two marked graves in their trail now. Strange and sad isn't it, that the only graves Dhorena had marked were for those who had no name? What the name of Dhorena's mother was is lost now to all but her, all but us. We know her name, I've sewn it scatter-like through my telling—do you recall what it was? You don't need to. For this story she don't need no name. None of them do, really. All that matters is that she lived and then she died in a time and way that was not to her liking and she had a daughter who likewise wished her mother had done her living a mite longer.

During those days, Knalc didn't speak with Dhorena at all—part because he didn't think she'd much welcome his words, and part because he didn't have any. There are words to share with those who have lost someone—but those words change from soul to soul; one wrong word and your pity births a quiet scorn. And

Knalc did feel pity.

He and Red hadn't grown quite kin-close in their time, but you don't fight shoulder to shoulder with a man, hunt with him for a season, and then feel nothing when you bury him.

After her two night wake, as the sun was setting and signaled what would have been her third night, she rose. Without word or whisper, she walked over to Knalc's fire.

Juices from rabbit meat dripped into Knalc's beard as he watched her coming.

She sat beside him. For a few breaths, he feared she was about to draw steel on him. But she didn't, she just picked up one of the other rabbits he'd skewered and started eating—driven by hunger. Though she must have been starved, she ate slow and reluctant, like food didn't do much for her no more.

The fire in her was faded. She was tired now. So tired.

They finished eating at almost the same time and sat with the songs of the Wilderlands around them. She put her head on his shoulder.

"He left us." She was not prompted to begin speaking and he had no reason to expect it, or even deep want to hear it, but he let her speak and speak she did. "It was years ago. Back when he had a name and wore a green coat and was called Mayn of Illmiv. He and a patrol would go out into the Wilderlands to cut new trails and find new plants and creatures for food and clothes and medicine. I was too little to know it then, but I'm told he was great at it. That he balanced the work of Mayn and Forage Captain like no one had ever seen.

"Then, in later years, he started to slip. Nothing that seemed to be calling anything into question—a man slipping a little after years of overwork. She stepped in to take up some of his duties as Mayn. Slowly, she found herself taking up all of those duties, and he would go on longer and longer excursions even though he and his team were bringing back less and less.

"I'd go so long without seeing him. And when he was back, half the time, he would come home during the night and the only sign he had been back would be the shouts sometimes waking me in my room and my mother's red eyes in the morning. I think by the end I resented him more than even she did.

"I still know he was wrong to desert us, but I can't help but think about how as he came home less and less, we were less and less warm toward him, which made him less likely to come home, which made us resent him even more.

"So there came a time he went out with a group of men and he didn't come back at all and neither did his men. We went over a year without hearing from him. My mother was named Mayness with full authority until he was found. She was more stressed, more worried in those first few months, but by the time seven months had passed, I think we were all happier for the most part.

"When they finally found him, crawling through the Wilderlands, he was a curse. He was the only one still alive of his men. They say the gods of the Wilderlands took his mind and made him murder his men—he'd said his men had all turned on him and tried to kill him, to stage a coup. In court, my mother asked him why—after all of his men were killed—didn't he come right back home? And he had no answer. He muttered about weather, terrain, the hardships of living, but he'd been gone a year and he was only fifteen miles from the city when they found him.

"My mother actually asked them to only strip him of title or place him on probation—but the judge, Zacharie, he'd never much liked my father, I'm told, and had him stripped of stature and soul and had his name struck from the stone that lists the Maynes of Illmiv and sentenced him to serve and protect the family he had abandoned. We got a protector after losing a father—my mother had noble blood, but between a disgraced husband and a mute child, we were severely diminished compared to where we had once been. I don't regret hating him for that. He wasn't my father anymore, they told me, because my father had died in the Wilderlands … I wasn't supposed to acknowledge that he was my father, or call him by any name, and I didn't want to. I hated him until I learned not to because I told myself he was less than human and what was the point of hating a person who isn't a person. What's the point in hating a thing? I …"

She was still too bone-dry to have tears to cry. Knalc lent her his water skin, she took it, sat up, and drank deep.

He let her breathe some, and when the water had done its work, he let her cry.

"I'm sorry," he said. "I'm sorry your mother's dead. I'm sorry it's by my hand. I'm sorry all you got is me."

These last words made her cry more.

Knalc nodded.

Now Knalc ain't no teller … but each of us has one story that we tell better than all others, so I'll keep this tale the same as Knalc worded it, for he knew it best.

"You wondered how I knew Valforian tongue a while back," he said. "Answer is, I learned it from my wife. This story is like to make you hate me deeper—but wait 'til the end, you're like to hate me different at the end than you do at the start."

He paused long and hard—the Wilderlands filled the space— and then he began.

"When I was younger—maybe half the winters I'm at now, maybe less than half—I was on a raid. It wasn't my first time going, but it was a good raid—every year, right after winter-start, you Valforians send all sort of food and goods and the like between your cities for celebrations. Most of those caravans you send are heavily guarded, but you got so many, not all the caravan masters can afford the steel to see them safe. Food is hard to find when the snow comes, so if we raid just one of these it's always cause for a safer winter for us. Usually you all have fewer mouths to feed, so it's not as if you'll miss the food.

"This all happened far south of here, probably a little before you were born.

"It happened that, on this winter-raid, I ran shoulder to shoulder with my brothers in the Khar clan—young and made of hotter blood and more brutish bits than I am now. I slaughtered soldier and traveler, grown and young, hound and human without discrimination. Some god of war and death may have touched me to be so battle hungry, so blade strong … or it's just as like I was crueler and more ready to be blood wetted then.

"The raid came to an end and we gathered those who had survived—none of the ones who I'd crossed of course, since in those days … and often enough still … those who crossed me didn't live. Most of those that lived were women and children, and since I was the most blood drenched with the least injuries, Gor Gamak let me have my choice of the unclaimed captives.

"She was the color of Grandma Dirt, a rare shade with you Valforians, with the make of Mamma Moon in her eyes. She was the only one who didn't look scared. Harking back now, I think she must've been, but if she was, she didn't look it. I chose her and declared I would make her my own wife. I know it's really nasty to think on. Being marriage bound to a bloodthirsty captor. But I didn't care.

"That night in my tent, I asked her why she didn't seem scared. She didn't answer. She didn't even look at me. I asked her again and still she didn't say nothing. I asked her a third time, and she just up and went to sleep.

"I was furious! My blood was hot and my mind was rage lathered. I waded through the Wilderlands, hunting coywolves and laughing-cats for sport.

"I came back at sunrise and found her in my tent. Not crying, just stoic and sitting there. I thought she must have been dumb. I yelled at her, 'What's wrong!?' and she just whispered something in a tongue I didn't understand.

"I stormed out of there—but the word she spoke was stuck on my tongue, and I repeated it over and over as I thundered through the camp. I asked some of my clan-kin what the word meant and none of them knew. That night, when I came back to the tent, I yelled at her:

"'*What is that word you said? What is* 'murderer?*"*

"And she just pointed at me.

"I told her that wasn't my name—I told her what my name was, then I pointed at her and asked her what her name was.

"'Prisoner.'

"And that's what I called her, thinking it was her name for almost a full season. 'Prisoner, *why didn't you look scared that night?*' and 'Prisoner, *why do you speak so little?*' and 'Prisoner, *where do you think you are that you can sit unwinced by my words?*' I was always so mad at her that I never spent any time in my tent, I'd be there for but a few breaths and then I'd storm out angry. I'd sleep under the stars or under Wilder-top—wondering what happened behind her eyes to make her so fearless.

"I don't know what it was. Part of me wants to think that she appreciated that, though I yelled at her, I had given her distance … but probably not; probably she was sick for any other soul to speak to.

"I came back once and she said something to me—this almost made me angrier, since I still couldn't understand her. But by now I was so hungry to know what made her fearless, that I made myself calm.

"We started trading words. I'd give her a Wilder-word and she'd give me a Valforian word. After a year of this, we were able to brokenly speak to one another.

"'Prisoner,' I would say. 'Why stay in tent?'

"'*Don't much like it,*' she'd say. '*Outside bad, Murderer.*'

"'Prisoner, why do Valforians use strange tongue?'

"'*Murderer, why do Wilderfolk speak strange?*'

"'Prisoner, night we met, why were you fearless?'

"'*Murderer,*' she said. '*I should say,* Prisoner *ain't my name.*'

"'*… What do you mean?*'

"'Prisoner *is what I am, not who I am.*'

"I was confused, so we talked some more as I puzzled out what a prisoner was with her and found out, by the end of that night, that her name was Octavaa. Though I never did ask her again why she wasn't frightened that night. With time now, I think I can figure why she wasn't scared that night. Some would say her gods hardened her heart to a fearless stone, but I think she was scared and scared to show it. Probably best that way. Had her fear been evident and I had picked her, I don't know what would have happened … that ain't true, I can guess what would have happened, knowing who I was back then.

"We lived like that for a time, trading our tongues, and I came to love her I think.

"I like to imagine she came to love me too. But it's just as like she didn't and was putting on a face, or maybe even she thought she did but her bones knew what might have happened if she didn't love me. It's a nice lie to believe she loved me; leastways it's nice for me.

"Most time passed like this. Two winters after that raid where we met, her stomach swelled heavy with child and soon I had a son. His name was Knoctin. He was the most beautiful thing I've ever held in my hands.

"And we lived the three of us, happy—or I was happy and Octavaa seemed happier than she had been long as I'd known her. Then one night, not much later, when my son was still just a suckle on her breast, I woke to an empty bed in the middle of autumn. Octavaa was gone and so was Knoctin.

"Frenzied and frightened, I took to tracking them down. I woke my friend, Giemar, to ask what had become of her. He said he'd only seen a shadow in the night he thought was some runt of a skunkbear wandering Wilder-ward. I would have run any way he pointed me then, but he was a true friend and he pointed me true.

"I don't know why she was so deep in the weeds of the Wilderlands. Maybe the child had crawled off while I slept and she had gone to find him. Maybe the Skin Serpent had beckoned to her in the night … Maybe she was running herself back to her real home with our child. I never got to know why for sure.

"I don't know how long I was running or screaming or looking. I don't think I would have stopped if I hadn't found them, but I did—backed against a rock by a pack of coywolves. I had my blade and I fought them off. Normally you can scare coywolves easy, once you slay or wound one or two of them they want to leave as bad as you do—but some mad god must have gotten into them … or, might be, they were just hungry. Most like they were just hungry and ready to die if it meant they might fill their bellies for just a day or two. I fought them off best I could, but that didn't amount to as much as I needed.

"In the midst of fight and fang, I grabbed Octavaa and we ran and ran and ran until we came to a cliff drop. I tried to turn back, to change course, but the coywolves were right on our hinds. I put her behind me as I brandished my blade.

"I fought them all through the night, slaying dozens I think, until there was one left. He was ancient without being old, scarred without being damaged, starved without being weakened. That coywolf charged and knock me back so hard I fell into Octavaa.

"I thought she tumbled over the edge, but she was dangling there, holding on to her life by a root in one hand, and holding on to our shrieking Knoctin in the other. I reached and tried to grab her but couldn't fight off the coywolf and pull her up at the same time. She would have had to drop the baby and take my hand with both of hers to get back to the safe side of the cliff.

"As my fight went on, she was starting to slip. I knew if I pushed the baby out of her hands, I could wrangle her back up without much trouble. She was starting to slip. And I couldn't bear the thought of pushing my son to his death. So I seized Knoctin and pulled him up just as Octavaa fell … I screamed and ran from that old coywolf clinging my son to my chest, salt flying from my eyes. I'd been chased so hard, fought so long, and was delirious with the death of my wife, I didn't realize I'd been running the wrong way until a day later.

"At sunrise Knoctin started wailing harder than he had been before, clawing at my chest. I guessed he missed his mother as I missed his mother.

"Late into that day I realized what Knoctin was really wailing about. That's when I realized the mistake I'd made in my saving: I had no milk to give him.

"I had saved the babe because my son was younger and had a life ahead of him, because I had more freshly gained him than her, and I knew if I saved her and not him I would lose any love she might have for me, but she couldn't fault me for saving our child.

"I didn't worry though, because I knew I could hunt and live in the Wilderlands. I could survive long enough to get him back to my camp where a woman of ample bosom could feed him proper.

"But he didn't stop crying. He didn't understand why I couldn't feed him.

"I was getting hungry and babe cries scare off prey and draw predators. I couldn't hunt and found myself evading hunters more than all else. Nearly six starving suns passed before I had to do it. Sometimes I wake up, babe-wailing myself, frightened that it was less than that.

"I had no strength. I had no rations. And I was alone in the Wilderlands."

Tears lit by firelight dripped down Knalc's cheeks like blood, falling into Grandma Dirt, who gobbled them up drop by drop. Dhorena listened. The Wilderlands watched as they always have. Words came out of Knalc's sorry throat more cracked than the clay hanging near his heart.

"I cooked and ate my own flesh and blood.

"It stopped the wailing. It stopped the hunger. It stopped me sleeping sound.

"I know the kinds of stories Valforians tell about Wilderfolk. I know you think we're all monsters that eat our children when it suits us. We don't … or, I guess, they don't … I did. Most Wilderfolk consider it an affront to the gods to eat human flesh—mostly I think they say that 'cause they don't like to think about some of us eating others.

"I found my way back to my clan's camp two days after that—too sprout-spined to let myself die in the Wilderlands. I told them all that my wife and babe were dead when I found them. I told them that the coywolves had picked clean both their bodies and prayed they couldn't smell the babe on my breath. They didn't and everything went back to normal.

"I eventually went back to where she died. It wasn't that far away—proper rations and keeping out an eye for directions, it wasn't that hard to find again. I found the cliff and charted a path down it, winding and winding down. At the bottom I found her body—already rotting and picked apart. I burned what was left and gathered the ashes in a clay sphere. I don't know if she loved me—but I know she didn't love the Wilderlands. She wouldn't want what was left of her scattered there. I can't help the rations that were picked up by coywolves and other foul creatures, but I can help this little bit. I swore to myself that one day I'd bring it back to one of the walls and scatter it behind them, that way she could be home again … least a little bit.

"So I took my shameful body, I took her ashes, and I took my memories and I hauled them all back to camp, back to normal. Hell-spat and horrid. I had seen my wife die and everything went back to normal. I had eaten my own son and everything went back to normal.

"And everything's been back to normal for seasons and moons too many. Too many to count, too many to care.

"It don't mean I didn't do it," Knalc said. "Eat my boy or kill your mother. I never wanted to kill anyone … that's a lie. Most of my life I've had a hankering for blood and battle, but after that, not so much. After that, I never wanted to kill again. But I was good at it, and I needed to live, I needed to do it both times to keep from dying. And I've killed a lot outside of that too, but only ever to keep from dying … I think."

They sat with that.

She didn't forgive him, she couldn't even if she wanted to. She couldn't bring herself to look at him, which is just as well since he couldn't make himself lift his eyes to her.

She didn't draw blade on him, though he'd confessed to being a monster of more malicious make than any she had fought afore. She didn't shrink from him, leer or sneer. She and he just stared at the fire, thinking on things that might have been.

I've told this story more than a dozen times afore this. I know the tale of Knalc's life like the back of my hand and I still can't find it in me to forgive him half the sins he had rotting inside his sorry soul.

After that talk, Dhorena understood him—enough, at least. Though understanding ain't forgiveness.

# XXI

YOU'VE ALL GONE QUIET. No muttering among you?

Many of you've heard this tale afore; no reason to clamp up now. I like the mutter of people under my tellings. If I'd wanted the whistle of winter wind under my words I could do my tellings to mountains.

But listen how you will I suppose. We're all worried about our hunters, caught now in the night.

Mark me here—call it a bone-hunch—but we'll see that party back before the dawn comes. I feel it. I say, I feel it …

My throat is going scratch-sore. We're nearing story's end now, so settle for the final stretch and I'll weave it for you to a proper close.

Knalc and Dhorena made their way to the four-headed god the next morning, leaving Red's grave and the tales they'd swapped behind 'em, never to be spoken of again. Dhorena's leg had healed right, whether time or Mist or the green-sick she'd had healed it was hard to say—point being, she was able to walk fine and kept good pace with Knalc.

They'd walked half the sun shift toward the four-faced god afore Knalc spoke the first words of the day. *"You know which way we're going?"*

Dhorena looked up at the four-faced god. *"Yes. I think I know it from here. I can see the faces of the Founders."*

Knalc hummed low. *"Founders? We call them the four-faced god. A god of four sides—valor, word-wit, courage, and honesty. When that god betrayed the morals that made up his faces, the other gods went against him and turned him to stone—now he makes up Hush-bee Mountain."*

"No," Dhorena said, no conviction in her voice, sounding sad even. *"I was always told that those were the men who founded the Valforian cities—Gregus, Alelex, Roovs, and Aleinc. Each of them founded one of the five cities of the Valforians and then came here to found Illmiv."*

Knalc nodded. *"Different from the stories I've heard. We do have an Alelex though. Alelex Who-Killed-The-World, who got the wrath of the Green God called down on all of us. Think they're the same?"*

She shook her head. *"I couldn't say. I don't know … do you think either of our stories are true?"*

Knalc sighed and spat. *"If you're not right and I'm not right—I don't know where that leaves us."*

"The wrong place," she muttered.

You might have thought it nice to see them both walking as they were. So long had she been wading through the Wilderlands that Dhorena almost looked more Wilder-bred than Valforian-born. Looking on her and him from a distance, you might have thought them father and daughter.

She led them on, in a dead-line to Hush-bee Mountain, knowing once she was square in its shadow she could better find the best approach to Illmiv. That walk burned them through the rest of Pappa Sun's shifting; when neither of them staggered nor spoke of making camp, they walked through Mamma Moon's shifting too without thinking or blinking of sleep. When Pappa Sun came running again 'cross the sky, they found lit afore them a stretch of land with bodies scattered within seein' of the Road.

Three bodies to count them true. Coming closer, they could see the dead numbered two men and one woman.

Standin' over them, they knew they were two Valforian men, by their cunning-made metal armor, and one Waste-Goddess, who they knew by the powder yellow paint coloring her milky torso, now blood-broken.

They were fresh out of the Wilderlands—only scattered trees in front of them and the Road in the distance, then some hills and not much longer until the walls of Illmiv.

They say the Valforians had to march down their Road every moon changing with axes and scythes to keep ol' Green from swallowing up the Road. That seemed true enough to Knalc as he could spot roots and vines and weeds reaching out of the Wilderlands toward the Road like fingers clawing for food—ready to seize it when most opportune.

There was no clear sign of the other Wastefolk.

"What do you think happened here?" Dhorena asked as they came upon the bodies.

Knalc drank in the sight.

A goddess on her own was a strange thing. It had already been strange to see them wander into the Wilderlands, but to come this close to a Valforian city was blue-strange to be sure. He kneeled down and looked closer at that Waste-god. She was stabbed thrice through her gut. Her hands were bound by thick vines.

"She was left here," Knalc came to. *"She must have used what Waste-magic she still had to kill these two men. Her followers must've tied her and left her at the roadside to die … she's still got shallow breath in her."*

"Why would they do that?" Dhorena asked.

"When people stop liking or believing in something—they're like

as not to tear it down." Knalc nodded to the men lying near. *"What can you say of these two?"*

"Soldiers," she said without having to look long. *"They were on patrol, like as not, and came across her. Depending how long they've been gone, they could send more to look for them soon since these two didn't come back."*

The bosom-goddess opened her eyes—

She took a screaming breath—

She seized Knalc's arm—

She tried to speak the mad-tongue of her people.

"I ain't got a good taste for your tongue," Knalc told her, hand on blade—ready if she tried to work any wickedness on him or the girl.

The goddess spat blood and clawed at him.

"Please …" she spoke Wildertongue with a strange flavor, but Knalc could decipher it well enough. *"Please … don't let me die …"*

Though he'd seen 'em, Knalc glanced down at her wounds again and shook his head. "No doing that. I'm no healer, not to human or god."

Tears and blood intermingled as they often do with the dying. Her claw-clutching was getting fainter. *"Please … Goddess lost followers … I'm like to burn … hell-sun … my soul … please … I do not want … I do not want …"*

Knalc could do nothing but listen and shake his head, so he granted the dying goddess that at least. But as he listened to her, his ears weren't strained for other sounds or shifting.

But Dhorena heard—Dhorena saw.

The bosom-goddess wasn't the only one who still had life left in her. One of the Valforians had kept himself soul-latched long enough to start crawling now. Crawling toward Knalc.

Dhorena didn't say anything. Just watched as the soldier moved across the ground on his belly toward the man and the pagan-goddess. As he crawled, he grabbed a sword—maybe his, maybe that of his battle-brother—and still Knalc did not notice. And still Dhorena watched.

"Please …" gargled the dying god. *"Worship me … my soul … might live well … please …"*

Knalc didn't have words or worship to give her, just the sorrow of a single sigh.

The blow came so quick, Knalc didn't even know what had happened.

Dhorena moved fast.

Her father had been a fighting man—he'd taught her how to hold her own against any sort of soldier—so she knew where the slips and creases were in the fire-folded steel of Valforian-made armor. Quick as lightning—easy as sin—she slipped her blade through the soldier's side.

She pulled it out quick and struck again at the other side just as smooth.

I can't prove it, but I reckon both that man and the bosom-goddess died in the same breath. Knalc missed both of their dyings as he turned, flabber-jawed to see Dhorena standing behind him—father's blade in hand and dying soldier underfoot.

Can you imagine a thing like that? Just a tumble from her home and she was killing clan-kin to save the likes of Knalc.

As blood dripped from her father's blade—her blade now—she and Knalc looked down on the dead with each other. Dhorena found friendly flesh at her feet, ready to turn to rot and worm food after committing the cardinal sin of obeying the only truth he'd been taught; Knalc saw a bosom-goddess limp in his arms—her milky eyes empty and staring at heavens she died thinking she'd never reach. Gods and mortals don't die as different as some other tellers would have you think, eh?

Wilderfolk and Valforians don't kill so different either.

Quickly, Dhorena wiped the blood from her blade and set it back on her belt.

"You ready?" she asked, turning back toward the Road. *"We're almost there."*

Knalc didn't speak or question her. He just lowered the now dead goddess into the grass next to the soldiers. A dunder-lout at a distance might have thought they were looking at lovers, Valforian and Wastefolk lying adjacent one another in the grass. I don't think such a thing has ever happened.

As Knalc walked away with Dhorena—toward the Road—he looked back at the sight, at the bosom-goddess, bleeding in the shade of the four-faced god. One dead god givin' shade to another.

Knalc looked away and walked on, his journey almost done.

XXII

THEY WALKED AS FAR AFTER that as they could on the Road 'til they were near enough to the city that horseback riders were sent out to meet them, kicking up dust in their wake. Maybe a dozen men, all decked in armor, riding battle ready steeds.

Knalc rested his hand on hilt, but didn't draw blade.

"You should talk to them," he said. *"They won't mind a lick of whatever words I spit."*

She nodded, stepped in front of him, and cleared her throat. "Soldiers!" she shouted. "I am Dhorena, daughter of two Maynes of Illmiv! I am daughter of Gloria! Daughter of Nicholus! Sister of Amok! I am returned from the Wilderlands, alive!"

They were still coming up on them fast, so she waited a bit before yelling the words again. "Soldiers! I am Dhorena Innauj! Last of my line—my forefathers diagrammed the walls that keep us safe and have long protected them as Maynes of the city. I have come back from the Wilderlands! I ask you, slow your speed!"

Maybe it was they couldn't hear her—but it almost seemed they rode faster.

Knalc's fingers tightened on his blade without drawing, though his muscles ached to for their own defense.

Even Dhorena's hand rested wary on her own sword hilt.

She waited, the Wilderlands behind her. There was no Wilder-laughing to ramble over her words.

She waited until the men were close enough they had to hear her for certain.

"Soldiers! I am Dhorena Innauj! This is my companion. We mean you no harm. I am the daughter of—"

And then the men were upon them with steel. Battle shouts and war screams bursting from their lungs as fury burned across their raised swords.

Dhorena and Knalc both had their own blades in hand fast as you could think.

Shoulder-side, they faced those charging, mounted men.

The first man at the head of the attack waved his sword—whooping wildly—more trying to run them down than cut them up.

Knalc and Dhorena dodged opposite ways—her blocking some stray steel as she did and him running his sword through the guts of the horse.

Gore spray-sprinkled the roadside as the horse shuddered, shambled, and fell—its rider likewise crumpled to the ground. Before he could find feet or wits, Dhorena plunged her sword through the slit in the soldier's steel and made it so he'd rest where he was a while longer while Death came for him.

Yet still eleven riders came.

Four went behind them, trying to circle-stick 'em—two foot-fighters being circle-stuck by riders was a fast way to die if ever there was one, both Knalc and Dhorena knew this. She moved fast to take the little cover the fallen horse could offer. She seized the knife of the fresh-killed soldier and threw it at one of those garish riders.

Her aim was off and the knife missed his nose but left him with a silver-tongue of muting sort. He sang a gargling tune as he fell off his horse to the ground—if not dead then wishing bad to be.

Mean time in front, two men—each with spear—came charging at Knalc, poised to run him through his heart. Knalc didn't have any sort of liking for that.

Fastlike, he belted his blade and grabbed both the spears by their shafts. Metal and wood burned his hands as he pulled both the tips into the other's horse. He and the men all collapsed and tumbled to the ground—one of the soldiers broke his neck in that fall.

The horses thrashed, and though Knalc was able to dodge their full might and keep from being fumbled, a lesser hoof blow left his shoulder bruised and bloody. Knalc tumbled to the dirt.

Seeing what happened, Dhorena acted quick-like, finding those secret armor folds in the soldier whose neck was still working right and saw to it that his kidneys didn't.

And nine men still swooped down on them

The three to their back were coming up fast and the five to the front saw Knalc was ground-bound for the moment and rode at the chance to slay him.

Dhorena saw this blood-hungry charge and drew her knife and sword-blade and leaped to battle with both brandished. Knalc saw the men who lusted to kill him and her and took two halves of the broken spear and vaulted to his feet, waiting for them to come to him.

With wood and steel and tooth and flesh, they fought off their attackers.

Oh, better than fought them off, children.

You ain't never seen blood run the way it did that day—turning the Road red as rubies in the sunset. If you wandered by the old spot, you can still see the stain where they fought. So much blood was spilled there that even Grandma Dirt can't lap it all up and grass grows red around it.

I could tell you that each of those men fought hard and long, fought for the one who warmed their bed back behind the walls. I could tell you that when Dhorena's steel sliced through skin and shields of the soldiers who had once protected her, she found the killing hard even as her knife moved easy into flesh and her sword severed bone with bliss. I could tell you Knalc thought of some of the men as coywolves and that made them easier to slay; some of the men he thought of as himself, and they were dead afore he could do all he wished to them. I could tell you the last man was Chirsic Holland—Dhorena's godfather—that she did not recognize him in his thick blue armor and he, mayhap, did not recognize her with the filth of the Wilderlands clinging to her and the blood of her kin painted on her face; I could tell you that Chirsic fought her and him and would have killed 'em both if Dhorena hadn't recognized a tricksy sweep he'd taught her and she'd replied with a muscle move that killed him and she only noticed her own knowing when she was already pulling her father's blade from his neck.

I could tell you anything you like and who's to correct me? All of them who might fact-fix me are dead now. But I'll tell you true and I'll tell you this—the ending stays the same: no men stood against them once they were done.

At least for a few breaths.

As they stood there, red, bleeding, and panting hard, they heard more horse-hooves coming near on the Road.

Both the blood weary fighters turned, ready to melt back to battle-minded things. The blood that covered 'em faded from thought, the bones around 'em crumbled from memory. They were not blade or body or bloody aim, they were creatures fighting only to breathe now and breathe again.

"Dhorena?"

She faltered, her eyes narrowed but her blade did not go lower. "Yes. I am Dhorena."

The man on the lead horse held a hand to his chest. "Captain Calium. I served … under your mother while she was Mayness. Your caravan is many months overdue." The silence you only find out of the Wilderlands filled the dead air between 'em. "What are you doing?"

She looked down at the bodies at her feet. Kin killed.

She looked up and saw Captain Calium looking at her, a dozen more men at his back—horror-slapped.

"We saw the fighting back from the wall and were dispensed to aid," the captain said. He then looked at Knalc—huge and heaving as he was—blade and brow both bloody and brutish from the burden of his work; Knalc traveling with a girl who had had a family and now had nothing but sword and knife. "Dhorena. Come away from him."

The men and their horses began to ease around them now, all ready with spears. Knalc and her too battle-spent to hope to fight them off, even if they thought different.

"No," Dhorena said. "Listen to me. Take me back. Let him go, understood?"

The captain shook his head. "He is responsible for killing some of my finest men. By rights I should kill him now where he stands as satisfaction. No, we're bringing him with us. Both of you."

One of the soldiers slid from his horse and walked toward her, reaching to take away her sword.

She flinched away and made sure he got a better view of her steel. "Come closer! *I'll gut you like an uggerfish.*"

He held his arms up and looked to his captain for guidance.

"I'll chalk that up to some sort of Wilder-sickness. Please, my girl, be compliant."

She shook her head. She might have lost her wizard-green, but the Wilderlands were bubbling inside her. "I keep the sword. It was my father's."

Captain Calium cringed. "You have no father, dear."

For a flicker, she considered throwing the sword through his neck, instead she burned hatred toward him after he spoke so hard he must've felt as if there was a blade aimed at his throat.

"I keep my sword," she said slow-like. "And my knife. I won't hurt anyone else, but the first one who tries to take either of those from me—or to kill this man—answers to me and my blades."

The captain chuckled as if to show his men how silly small girls can be—but from the way he glanced and tugged at his armor, he had half a gulp of fear in his gullet.

"If you must," he said—chortling too much.

"I will," she said, keeping her steel brandished.

"Very well, you will ride with me, and that mongrel—"

"No," she said.

The captain stopped—he cleared his throat. "Pardon?"

"The mongrel and I," she explained, "will be given a horse by you, which you may lead if you wish."

Oh, that captain didn't shine well to that idea. "We would, my dear," he said, then motioned to the dozen horses dead and dying on and 'round the Road. "Except if we trusted you near another horse, we'd be rather worried you'd kill it."

She didn't even look at the beasts around her whose blood painted her the color of hate and lust, the color of fire and clay. "We won't. And we won't leave. If we do, you'll be able to catch us and bring us back."

"This will not be acceptable," the captain chuckled too much again, looking at his soldiers as if this look could make false words true. "You will both be sharing horses. More specifically, you will share my horse and this creature you picked up will be bound and led behind."

Dhorena didn't flinch and didn't hesitate. "You will give us a horse which we will both ride back. This is what will happen if you want me to come quietly."

The captain growled lightly and narrowed his eyes. "Are you threatening me?"

Her voice was still as winter-water. "I am observing how events will likely transpire under a variety of circumstances and sharing my insight with you. You're welcome."

The captain mulled that over for a mite, then nodded to one of his soldiers. "Bradaal—off your horse."

Bradaal, less man than boy, turned pale. He took a look back at the cast of soldiers and then to his commander. "Sir?"

"You heard me," Calium said.

"I'd be walking all day to get back, sir."

The captain gave him nasty eyes and a stonewalled mouth of teeth through which he hissed. "Then you best get off now and start walking so that you get back behind those walls before sunset."

With the zeal of a scorned child, Bradaal slunk from his saddle, walked his mount over to Dhorena, and started trudging horizon-ward to those walls.

Trying as best she could to not look away from the captain, Dhorena got saddle settled, then motioned to Knalc to do the same.

The Wildman still had his blade drawn, still was ready to—at a breath—lurch into a kill-shower.

"*Come on,*" Dhorena said—she hung her blades from her belt and held out a hand to him. "*Please.*"

Knalc fingered the cracked clay sphere hanging 'round his neck—the albatross that kept him breathing. The thundering of his recent fight was still making a racket in his chest, truth be told, but the contents of the clay were smooth and calm. Slow-like, he put his own blade to belt and got on the horse behind her.

"We're ready," she told the captain—who snorted, but didn't sass none. He pointed four of his men to ride behind Knalc and her, while he and two more led the way.

They took off toward the walls, passing Bradaal in a hand-set of hoof beats.

Knalc and Dhorena whispered to themselves some as they went.

"We should have fought them," Knalc said. *"Found another way in after-wise. We already slain a smattering of them, they're like to kill us for that."*

"They ain't gonna kill me," she said. *"And I'll see to it they don't kill you either."*

Her tone was so even it almost made Knalc think she was telling him true.

"Why you say that?"

"Because of who I am," she said. *"I'm the daughter of two former Maynes, they won't kill me unless I do something horrible."*

Knalc had to keep from laughing there. *"Because of who you are? Maybe it's just you ain't viewed yourself in your fancy Valforian glass late-like, but you're looking more Wilder than Valforian these days. Anyone in there taking passing glance to you would mark one more of my kin than theirs. 'Who you are' is a misguided girl."*

She shrugged. *"The blood that's in me beats out the blood on me."*

Hearing those words, Knalc began to suspect she was telling him right. *"I don't think I got quite as fancy blood in me as you do."*

"I'll talk to them. I've got blood enough for both of us. Do you still have it?"

His fingers closed again around his clay. He held it close to his chest—the ashes within it as cool and calm as ever.

"Yes."

They kept their route to those walls.

Those walls—ooh, imagine them now.

Many of you have seen their like. One of you has seen them true, I know you have—I had to hold you in my arms 'cause you were scared when we neared them—scared to walk in their shadow. You thought they would fall and flatten you. You're blushing now, but I'll grant you, them walls can be mighty frightsome. 'Course, to look at the walls now, you see only their crumbling skeleton. You see stone stacked as high as the tallest tree, broken only by a slouch or ravagers looking for good rock who don't know you lose more trying to mine pieces from that wall than you gain in the getting—unless you found a silver ring or a gold tooth while you were rummaging through those ruins.

Back when all I'm telling was still unfolding, them walls weren't just mighty—they were indomitable. Indomitable in breadth; if you put a hand to that wall and started walking, you could keep on walking and die of thirst before you came back around to where you started and barely find crack, crevice, handhold, or hollow. Indomitable in depth; it's said that, at its thickest, if you station one man at the top of the wall, looking out at the four-faced god and Hush-bee Mountain, you could line twenty more men behind him, loin to ass, and the last would still have farting room. Indomitable in might; Valforians have killed many Wilderfolk—in the Wilderlands, probably 'bout as many as Wilderfolk have killed Valforians—but in the shadow of that wall are graves so prolific no teller could sing the tales of all the Wilder-souls that suffered and perished in that shadow; no matter how well sung or long winded the teller, even just to sing all the names would take a life-time and that ain't even taking in the names of Wastefolk or the wizard army of Ammign who died against those walls.

Now it's ruins; but this story ain't happening now. Back then, it was something that could never have succumbed to magicks or the rot of ages.

Dhorena was born 'hind those walls in their prime. There was a time in her life when she'd wake and see grey stone more than she saw Pappa Sun. She'd known how to fear the wall for the tales she was told to frighten her about souls being sleep-called to curl up in it before turning to stone—but she'd never known how to fear it for the utter mass of wall there was to witness.

But now, after so long abound in the Wilderlands and without her wizard learning hiding her, she shook a little in fear as they neared that wall which—even 'cross from the visage of the four-faced god—seemed like a deity in its own right.

"Tell me, what's it like 'hind that mighty stone?" Knalc whispered to her, some flavor of fear leaking into his voice.

"You won't like it," Dhorena said.

Knalc clutched his clay tighter as he looked up at the walls, grey like cliff sides.

As they neared, the wall split open for them, the grinding of grates and gears and other ghastly crafts pried open an entrance, gaping like the mouth of a massive silver tip.

With soldiers leading them and soldiers at their rear and soldiers unseen on walls above them, they went through that gate. Like water over rock—one barely would have thought them prisoners to see how easy they flowed through.

Struggling and tantrums don't divert it. All things move toward their end.

XXIII

THIS WILL BE MY LAST time telling this tale. Call that notion another bone-hunch of mine.

I know it's late in the telling to thrust that on you all—but I don't reckon I'll have it in me to tell this story again. My tongue is growing thick, my words thin.

I'm not sure I'll have the fire in me to tell anymore stories at all after this one.

So mark my words well in your mind; maybe if some of you find some precious paper and ink, you might remember enough to mark it down there.

But don't mind my rambling. All tellers retire or die and often as not their words are lost or twisted—oftentimes even before they die their stories have been wrecked or warped. I don't expect to be any different. I'm old, tired—this tale always takes a chunk out of me.

I remember where I was.

Going through the gates of Illmiv to whatever waited behind that wall. The gate Dhorena and Knalc went through opened fast and closed faster, and they found themselves marching down a short, man-hewn tunnel.

As they did, Knalc had a quaking in his bones. Most of us get it once before we die: a moment where—without being bound to time or flesh—we see, clear as mountain air, the rhyming of things. Knalc was seein' just so.

As they passed through the tunnel—sneak-like—he pulled his clay from around his neck and put it around Dhorena's. She felt it happening, but didn't move to stop him.

"What's this?" was all she asked, knowing sure as sin what it was.

"No matter what happens," he said. *"I want you to crack that in the wind at the highest part of the city. I won't be able to get up there."*

She didn't say another word, just pulled that clay snugsome 'round her neck, making sure no harm would come to it while it was in her care.

A silent contract was sealed, and they emerged into Illmiv proper.

There wasn't a lick of green or honest brown behind those walls—just the grey of storm clouds and dead things. What colors there were had too bright a bend to them not to be false and poisonous. But the humans there must have been enough to make up for every animal their stone lives lacked. No wonder all attacks against those walls were fated to be broken. If Valforians ran out of the steel wielding type of man, they had more men of brawny-bod to snatch from their towns—they weren't left to pick from babes who couldn't even hold the word *"blade"* on their tongue. There were more men and women Knalc saw in his first few dozen gasps behind those walls than he had seen in any camp or battle-troop in Wilds, Wastes, or Road.

There were no Wilderlands there, but this stone and human habitat had a hum to it too. I suppose you could call it a lifesome hum too … only human yammering and the happenstance of barking or squawking from some bird and tame-dog.

Dhorena didn't flinch even as she heard people point at her and whisper her name. She'd forgotten, in all honesty, the clutter of human life inside the walls. She'd been born into it but after the long trek through the Wilderlands, this seemed a strange place. The faces of people—people she knew—like a forest around her. After so long outside the walls, her mind told her to suspect treachery, the work of wizards or tricksy gods. But no, all that she witnessed was the treachery of humans who'd holed up from gods and the rest of us.

Over cobble and brick, rock and mortar, they were led through crooked streets, past buildings sturdy as a thorn-horn's legs and a dozen times as tall. Buildings that would war well, but were used for bread baking and mead making and likewise things—most were just for living in, stony and impenetrable as they were. A fortress made by the gods themselves would be hard pressed to rival the work of meager man here—and though gods are made of mightier stuff than man, it shook Knalc to know what man might muster.

As they went on, he saw it: the Sword Tower.

Glass and stone reaching up and up and up, looking ready to scrape out the heart of Mamma Moon or Pappa Sun if one of them ran too close in their shifting. A sword that could kill a god were it not for the fact it was made for something as idle as men ruling over other men. Even from outside the walls, the tower could be seen—pointing toward the heavens like a challenge to the gods, none of whom would strike it down for fear their flesh would be rent in the effort.

By the time they were in the shadow of that edifice, the hum of humans had grown to the point of being almost unbearable to Knalc as he looked about him, overwhelmed by the spectacle of flesh on display—copious, unending, and hateful of him.

From the Sword Tower, a man emerged, walking toward them as the crowds gathered for the arrival of Dhorena and Knalc.

This man was Zacharie Reggil and he was a man of simple extravagance. If you'd just given him a walking-look, you wouldn't think he had wealth hoards more than many a man there. The simple band around his head was a gold purer than sunshine. His clothes were a more perfect purple than a dusk sky, but one would think them merely a flavorful black in passing. Rings adorned his fingers, but though the shape of those rings was not extravagant, the make of the metal was difficult indeed: platinum, silver, even sapphire, all magic-bent to be a perfectly smooth ring.

Dhorena came off her horse and Knalc followed after.

I'll tell you a secret—something even Knalc himself didn't know until that moment. He thought he'd be able to slaughter-slay his way from behind those walls if he needed to. He hadn't even told it to himself yet, but his plan had been to break his clay if he could and then escape by blade or blood or most like both. Now—for the first time—he was realizing that was impossible. He wasn't even sure he'd know how to run back to the gates they'd come in through, what with the way the streets and roads here had wound on. His hand was on his hilt, but he knew he could not draw blade to do more than peel his nails, because to do else would bring a fury-flood of human flesh down on him.

His hand waited on his sword.

"Dhorena!" Zacharie Reggil said, arms wide as he drew close. "You're alive!"

"I am." The girl seemed less than wonder-pecked to see him. Her arms were crossed and—like Knalc—she had a hand resting on her sword. Knalc also suspected that if it came to it, the flood around them would let her have better use of her steel than he would of his.

Zacharie bowed a little to her and then did the same to Captain Calium. "Wherever did you find her?"

"Standing over a troupe of our men in the middle of the Road—bloody as a newborn." The captain said, clearly soured by the memory.

That turned Zacharie a touch pale to think on. "Ah … I see." He smoothed his robes, though they were not wrinkled, and brushed dust off his sleeves, though they were not dirty. "I'm sure there will be much for us to catch-up on. First things first, of course. Kill this drooling savage."

A dozen soldiers crept toward Knalc—eight drew swords, the others pulled bows taught.

Steel sang—but it was not Knalc's. Dhorena stood in front of the man, brandishing her blade on his behalf—a fire lit 'hind her eyes. "No one will touch him."

The soldiers stopped and looked to Zacharie for his tell-to.

The Mayn bit his lip just shy of blood. "Dhorena, come away from him. He's little better than a dangerous animal."

She held her ground. "I'll kill the first one of you who touches him."

The crowd gathered tighter 'round them and gasped and shushed and gawked. A soldier would start to slink nearer only to have Dhorena bat at them with her steel.

"She's more like a dangerous animal if you ask me," some crowd watchers noted—seeing how she stabbed for blood and pain whenever she went for one of the soldiers.

"That's enough!" Zacharie held up a hand and his soldiers stopped. He sighed and rubbed his head. "Very well, bring the wretch to a cell where he will await his fate."

Nervously—the soldiers belted their swords and started to move toward Knalc again.

Dhorena didn't relent. One man reached to grab Knalc's arm and, were it not for his armor, she'd have cut hand from arm.

"*No one touches him!*" she hissed, loud enough for the city to hear. "He is the reason I have come back home. Were it not for him, I would have died three times over!"

All eyes looked to Zacharie. The city waited.

He showed the smile of an old man watching a babe not yet

tooth-grown try to chew on sticks and stones. "I am taking your request into account, Dhorena. However, this creature cannot walk the city free. We have women and children and men of tender make. I will put him in a cell and you and I will discuss this like civilized folks."

She kept her ground. She kept her blade in hand.

Again, the Mayn sighed. He waved his hand. "Take them both."

The soldiers began moving in again—weapons back in hand.

Dhorena's steel got to work.

She moved fast, enough that she'd have given her father a hard race. She seemed to be in as many as three places at once as she blocked the soldiers' approach. Stabbing and twisting, she left long scars on skin and armor plate alike. Her sword danced between her hands, left and right using it just as well between them to mark her enemies.

Whether they were shocked, or trying not to harm her, or she just out skilled them, the soldiers tripped and struggled against her.

One managed to draw a thread of blood across her left cheek and break for Knalc.

She rewarded him with a howl and a sword through his gut.

He managed to pull back from his charge before the steel could bleed him belly to back, but he stumbled away, sputtering and gasping. Blood flowed from between his armor plates. He clutched at his wounds, but couldn't reach them through his armor. He fell to his knees and then his side—blood pooling around him. More blood than most there had seen.

And Knalc just stood at the center of her flurry—unmoving.

Now the crowd was all gasps and shouts and jabber-jawing:

"She's the daughter of two Maynes!"

"Kill the Wildman!"

"She's just a girl!"

"Did she kill him?"

"Have some respect!"

"There's blood!"

The girl was good, there's no spitting on her skill, but even a skilled fighter is gonna turn tired after a time and that was already in the happening for her, moving fast and fierce as she was to keep all those men back.

Her bounds between the soldiers were getting slower and her slices less fierce and focused. People ain't perfect and all they had to do was wait for her to slip—which she did. She slipped on the blood of the man she had stabbed.

Cracked her head real good on the cobble too, the whole of Illmiv must've heard.

She was on her feet again fast though, even as her head drooled in a sanguine sort of way.

The soldiers didn't wait for her to find her fight-fire again. No sooner was she on her feet than a hunk of those men tackled her to the ground.

Knalc held his hilt, but did not draw.

When the soldiers reached him, he didn't fight much as they wrestled him to the ground and began to drag him away.

Silver tip and Mist and wizard—to be laid low by men whose names no one knew or cared to know. That's the way it is in stories more often than not. You live to slay a wyrm of worthy sort, but you best bet you'll be beaten by some half-blink beatnik down the line. That's the way of things.

Zacharie laughed a mite at their struggling. "Take the wretch to the dungeon. And take Dhorena to my chambers; we will talk and see if we can't navigate this unusual situation."

All that Knalc and Dhorena could do was watch the other be

dragged away, both pulled through different doors into the Sword Tower.

Some of you seem worried. I want you to know that they see each other again.

I want you to know that when next they meet, she finally gets her revenge.

XXIV

FIRE-WINE WAS POURED BRIM HIGH into a silver goblet for her.

She'd never had wine before and she sipped at it gingersome. It burned as it sleeked up her throat. Her mother had always told her she wouldn't like wine the first time she tasted it, but as she let it mull in her stomach, she found she had a tongue for it and took a heftier helping as she sipped again, deeper.

Zacharie Reggil, Mayn of Illmiv, watched her, probably wishing he'd slipped some poison into that cup of hers. If he wasn't wishing it then, he certainly would be soon after.

"We thought you dead," he said

She watched him watching her and took another deep drink, leaving her goblet half empty when she was through with her glug. "I don't blame you for that."

He smiled, thin and laugh-less. "Tell me what happened."

She reached for the goblet to get another glug of the good stuff, but found she was already a touch dizzy from the winespell. Instead, she reached for the boar—skinned and roasted and mouth-watering—at the center of the table. She took a good chunk out of it and started chomping and drooling. It had been a good few seasons since she had spice or seasonings or full meat cooked over a grand fire. She hadn't realized she was hungry until she'd sunk her teeth into it. She got started on a good gnaw before Zacharie cleared his throat.

He said, "I wonder: what happened to you out there?"

"Not enough to kill me."

"Charming." There was his smile again, it seemed to hurt his face to summon.

She was reaching for the bread, barbarously ripping a huge chunk from the whole. She stuck a healthy hunk of that in her mouth and nodded to her host. "I'm more interested in what happened to you. Last I saw you, you were just a judge."

Zacharie leaned back in his seat and folded his hands.

"The position of Mayn was still open after your mother was forced to vacate it. When neither she nor anyone returned from your diplomatic visit, it was assumed she was dead and her petition for reinstatement was dropped immediately. As head of the judges' bench, the position passed to me."

Dhorena sipped again from the fire-wine.

"I can't help but wonder what happened out there in the Wilderlands to make you feel the need to protect that creature."

"He protected me." She spoke without meeting his eye.

Zacharie made play at looking around the room as if searching for something, he shrugged when he couldn't find it. "I find it interesting that he protected you. What is it that you gave him? What is it you even had to bargain with? A young woman as you are, all alone in the Wilderlands."

Her hand clutched for her sword—but it had been taken from her before she had been seated. She didn't speak, she only stared him down.

The Mayn smiled and this one didn't seem to hurt, it spread over his face easy as lamb butter. "What is it you had that wasn't possessed by your bodyguard or the tongueless who traveled with you?"

Under the table, her hands raked against cloth and flesh for her sword, grasping so bad for it that, had she been able to seize and draw it, she might have used her own femur to bone-beat the man to death.

His words dug at her with the veracity of a man leaning into a dying enemy with a sword. "I assume that mutt you brought into our house killed both of them. I assume he told you he'd let you live. He said you were different, that you were kind to him, that you were innocent, soft, and sweet. I assume he said this after he killed your mother."

Her hands stopped clutching. Stopped because she had found steel.

Seizing the carving knife from the boar, she threw it at Zacharie.

The knife missed his left cheek by three hairs width.

"I challenge you, Zacharie," her eyes seared holes into him. "I challenge you for your title as Mayn."

He pulled the knife out of his wood chair and frowned. If his heart was hammering as it ought to have been, he had it buried good. "I'm afraid you're about two hundred years too late with your challenge. Duels for political positions have been outlawed."

"Unless the seat is held by two living entities, then one party may challenge the other should they refuse to cede it." She took a deep breath, readying her soul for the sting of the lie she wove. "My mother is alive in the Wilderlands. Her petition was successful. She is traveling behind us. She holds the rightful position and, on her behalf, I challenge you so that she may lawfully be reinstated to her seat. You and me in single combat at sunrise."

He turned the knife over in his hand. "Very well," he said. "While I don't relish killing a young woman, I will do what I must. I had hoped to cure you of your Wilder-madness, but if you will make me put you down like a rabid dog, I will do so. Killing broken souls brings no praise worth song or commendations."

"I survived the Wilderlands," she spat.

"No," he said, chillsome. "Some sickness has twisted the girl who was Dhorena into parlaying with a man who killed the members of her family she herself did not slay. You know you killed your own godfather on the Road here? Chirsic was in the first set of men dispatched to bring you back and now my understanding is he lies bleeding in some ditch.

"But by all means. I look forward to you trying to kill me too; but unlike you, I am not craving the blood I will have to draw to defend my title. Not because I think you do not deserve death as you are now. Not because you are less than a woman. No, it is because, unlike you, I flinch away from dealing death to others."

"Liar!" She slammed her fists on the table, rattling food and wine. "You killed my father! You took everything from him!"

"I upheld the law. His name was stripped from him when he abandoned you. I maintained our system of governance, my dear. I didn't kill your father. You think it murder? I think it suicide. Or incompetence. Take your pick."

She was reaching for another knife—a fork, a spoon—all she flustered at him with deadeye aim.

But he was fast for his year and caught or stepped past all she threw.

"Guards!" He shouted.

Dhorena flung herself out of her seat and charged him. Her thin fingers wrapped savagely around his neck. He had a head or two over her, but her muscles had grown in the Wilderlands, and her rage writhed ferociously in her gut. She tried, oh, she tried to wrestle him into the great fire that burned in that dining hall.

Had it been a day he were tired, she might have burned him there.

Had she spent a longer stint in Wilderlands, she might have burned him there.

Had a god of any make given her a nudge of might in her aim, she would have burned him there.

But the guards rushed to 'em—prying her fingers from his throat to reveal the gift she'd left him—a purple band about his neck to match the shade of his robes and the shape of his crown.

He gasped and gripped the new adornment.

One of the guards tried attending to him, but Zacharie quickly brushed him off. "I'm fine," he said. "I'm fine. What I need is for you to take Dhorena here to see the judges' bench—she wishes to move forward with a challenge of combat for position of Mayn. See that she registers her grievance and, following that, see that she is taken to her room and kept there until the morning. These challenges end in death or maiming, so please attend to her and ensure that her last hours of her current existence are comfortable. Or at least, have as much comfort as a mad beast can derive."

"You're a boar-fucking bastard, Zacharie," she spat as she was dragged out of the room.

"See that whenever she speaks that savage tongue, someone scours her mouth!" he shouted after as the doors slammed closed.

XXV

THAT NIGHT, WHILE MAMMA MOON was running frightful close to the Sword Tower, Dhorena climbed to its point.

The guards had locked her in her old room, the room she had grown up in. She knew every bend and trick to those four walls. They'd been smart enough to lock her window, but a brick in one of the corners had been loose for ages now. It was a tighter squeeze than she remembered, but she managed to slither out to the balcony below and make her way up the tower mite by mite.

She had been there many times before on clear nights like this, when she could see the shower of moonlight on the city below. The way the light of the moon glowing off stone and brick turned all of what was behind the wall to precious silver.

She'd climbed here when she was younger to try to catch glimpses of goings-ons on the far side of those walls; now she knew what waited out there was more horrible than all the concoctions of her young mind—and that was after only witnessing a thimble full of what the Wilderlands might spit at you.

She pulled the clay sphere Knalc had given her from her pocket—it was chipped and worn. It was, she thought, maybe not old but just looked it 'cause of the web of cracks runnin' 'cross its surface. But the cracks did not go core deep and the wear had not yet broken it.

Holding it up to the moon, she said a prayer, first to Aprheus, then to Wilder-gods, then to Aprheus again for safety, asking for forgiveness for praying to false gods and wishing that, this high up, Pearlaphine would have an easier time flinging Octavaa's soul heaven-ward.

Once her prayers were done, she raised the clay above her head.

The wind was gentle.

She pulled on the clay and found it broke easy in her hands. She marveled that it had held together so long.

The dust of the dead sparkled in the moonlight as it blew out from the Sword Tower over the city below.

The world around her seemed to sigh. Though what was dead had merely gone on, it felt as though something else in the world had died; and, as with all things that die or go, the world was not better or worse for it. Just different than it was before.

She had not known the woman, but Dhorena hoped Octavaa could rest easy now.

Dhorena herself did not know for certain which gods were worth worshipping or where the best place to stand in this word was. But having walked the Wilderlands, having been born under mightsome walls, she hoped that if Octavaa had some of her in both places then whatever soul might be scavenged from her disparate halves managed to end up mostly in the right place.

The night was cold, but Dhorena didn't notice.

She sat on the Sword Tower and dreamed of her home. Yes, she was already home, but it's always happier to live there in memories. She dreamed less of towers and walls, less of mobs and masses, and more of her mother, her father, her brother, back before this tale came to happening.

Meantime, deep deep under Dhorena, at the roots of the

Sword Tower, Knalc glowered in the dungeon.

He knew what a cage was. He'd seen and even made some with thick branches and ropes. He'd never been inside a cage, but he always thought he could rip or tear or beat his way out of one. But this was a cage of metal and even rusted as it was, it wouldn't budge by blow from foot or fist.

There's no way he could have known, but the same moment the clay cracked and his wife's ashes interlaced themselves through the city, through a place like their home, he felt a peace in his heart he had never felt before.

Clanless, clayless, cage bound.

He stopped his hammering against his metal bindings and let himself slip to the floor of that terrible cell.

Only one death left to witness.

He didn't sleep well, but his soul was sound.

XXVI

PAPPA SUN BROKE THE HORIZON with a burst of blood, and left a red trail behind him as he strode 'cross the sky.

Zacharie waited for Dhorena in the Challenge Ring, an arena at the rear of the Sword Tower where blood had not been spilled in two hundred years. He waited in armor made to dazzle and daze more than defend and deflect, but even then it looked like it could do deflecting finer than most armor makes. His long sword had more jewels than blood on it. Zacharie had been a warrior once in his youth. Not that he was old when this fight occurred … well, old by the living of Wilderfolk, but by Valforian living he was yet to crest half his life. Before he was Mayn, before he was a judge, he had killed men and beast and Wilder-things. Though time had tugged at his muscles some, his mind was keen as his sword and all that stood between him and blade mastery was some time to recount those old songs he'd sing with blood sopped steel.

Now, I could chew your ear off about what Dhorena had to do to get that Mayn to strut the street all war-clad, but I'll just give you what you need to know. How before this, Dhorena had put up her argument to a gaggle of judges, that she had to tell them of what had happened in the Wilderlands without giving 'way that her mother had died right at the start of the tale's telling. I'm not without my own swollen sense of self, so I don't mind saying that her word weaving would mark her a mightsome teller. The judges all gossiped and gandered at her even while she stood before them. Saying things like "Flummox the Well of the Ancients!" or "Walls be blast, we'd be listening to a babe!" or "By the hobbling of my wire face" or things that made as much sense as that. She ought to be thankful she has royal blood—though the royal never are, had she been a blood-drop more base-born, she would have been laughed right out of those chambers. It was by a beggar's hair that she got the permissions she needed to issue her challenge.

So now I come to the part I imagine you're listening for: the blood duel. That's what everyone in the city had gathered in the Challenge Ring for. Not long after Zacharie came out, Dhorena stepped to face off against him.

She had been given armor that fit her mostly fine, she'd been offered clothes of nice make, but she'd turned them down. She'd instead taken the clothes she had garnered in the Wilderlands and found a red jacket she knew in the castle and adorned them both.

You can't imagine the way the crowd gasped when she came out in that red jacket. The mark of high-born shame, of those who had committed sin so foul they lost their name. She didn't flinch at the crowd's yammering, just rolled and wrinkled the folds of the jacket so that it fit her better than it was made to.

An old man, ancient by Wilder-living, came from the bench of judges to announce the fight to the gathered crowd.

"We are here to witness the challenger," he faltered when he looked at her, as the red coat, by tradition, meant he was not permitted to breathe her name, but no name reaping had lawfully happened to her, "Dhorena Innauj, whose mother, our dear Mayness Gloria, was pushed from her position over two years ago. Dhorena claims her mother's petition was successful and that she is now in the Wilderlands, alive and making her way here.

Standing opposed to her is Zacharie Reggil, the current Mayn who is accepting her challenge in hopes of maintaining his claim to that same seat."

The old man took a moment and let the crowd cheer and boo and whoop and weep and yawn as crowds do. When their rattle had gone down to a simmer, the old judge bowed to both the fighters.

"Combatants, you may begin."

He stepped hurriedly out of the way before the fight went full flung.

The fight was over within thirty-seconds.

Next to silver tips, next to Knalc himself, next to the horrors of the Wilderlands, the unpracticed Mayn was nothing. His armor made him heavy, his visor made him mostly blind, and her father had once owned the armor Zacharie now fought her in. It was the trickiest to find the seams in, but it was the armor she had learned from.

She was upon him—fast as a thunder-snake—just as he prepared his jewely sword.

She slipped her mother's knife in that leg-seam. He staggered and cursed, falling to one knee.

She didn't even satisfy herself with a smile; she had butchery at hand. She moved behind him and wrenched off his helmet as he failed to get to standing full again. She could have driven her steel deep through his neck, but that would have been too easy. She made a shallow cut that would kill him, but slow-like.

He gargled something that could have been "I yield," but through his mangled blood leaking it could have just as easily been "You bitch."

It's the same sentence if you only count syllables.

Her sword moved and cut deep in his arm.

Then his other arm.

Then she wretched the blade from his leg-seam and pushed it into the other.

He wasn't even kneeling now, he was on the ground—cold and damp and without the means to beg or scream. Shaking with the fear of realizing Death was slouching toward him.

And then—knowing her blades couldn't make a clean cut anywhere else on his armor, she straddled him and, with her father's sword, made a hole in the back of his mouth.

Some say he stopped moving after that, others say he kept moving longer than a soul would want. If I tell you what I think, I think he'd stopped moving afore she'd dug her blade into her mark. I think he willed his soul from its shell before she could finish her work.

She stood and she walked away as the crowd stared at what was left behind her.

Someone started a cheer, but that died faster than Zacharie. Soon after, the crowd went shock silent. Dhorena couldn't say whether it was happening true or just her mind fooling with her, but it got so quiet, so still in Illmiv, she could swear she could hear the distant laughing of the Wilderlands from over the wall. And why shouldn't she have? The Wilderlands are growing ever closer. In a way of thinking, all those people had just seen the Wilderlands kill their Mayn right in the middle of their fortress. They watched the remains of Zacharie draining down the cobble and through the city.

Dhorena, covered in two shades of shameful red, looked at them all. She felt hollow now. She had killed the man who had stripped her father of rank with the sword of her father and the knife of her mother, but all it meant was another man dead; she had no comfort, just the blood covering her skin, growing colder by the heartbeat.

The judges' bench, which had been watching from their high podium, tried to send the same elderly judge back over, but he seemed too stirred up by what he'd witnessed to amble over. After some more gossiping and hissing, they sent over a woman of middling years.

The woman smiled forcefully, her eyes trying their darndest to focus on Dhorena, but always wandering over to the dead Mayn even as she spoke. "Congratulations," she said. "It seems you've won the trial of combat."

Dhorena didn't blink at her, even as blood ran 'round the rim of her eyes. This shook the woman, though she fought the urge to show it. The woman coughed some phlegm from her throat. "In light of your apparent victory, until your mother returns from the Wilderlands, law would typically dictate that you act as Mayness in her place. However …"

Dhorena's eyes went narrow. "Yes?"

How fast that old woman cast away her gaze. "However … myself, and the other judges as well, they are uncertain of your … mental state. We feel it would be best if one of us took up leadership until your mother returns."

Dhorena looked hard at that woman who wouldn't look none at her. "You're uncertain of my mental state?"

"We all are. Yes."

"Then why'd you let me fight a man to the death? I'm in a proper mental state to put my life on the line but not to lead?"

The judge didn't even try to hide the way she stared at Zacharie and then at Dhorena's blood glossed blades. "It is because of the result of the battle that we think you might not be in a sound state of mind."

"It was a battle," Dhorena said. "What happened to him is what happens in battles."

"… He yielded."

"Not the way I heard it," she said, not even thinking of the tongue she was speaking with.

But the judge noted it, sure as sin, and her eyes went wide, she nearly took a tumble as she stepped away from that gorish girl. "What? What did you say?"

From that fear-shot look, Dhorena realized she'd used Wilder-speak. She tried to offer a chuckle, to laugh it off, but that only coxed fear from the judge's eyes. And it was at the same time, she realized the masses and masses of people around her, all looking at her with fear. Hungry fear. I don't want to sit here preaching, pretending like they should have welcomed the girl calm and easy like a new-born babe, but a hungry fear is a need to snuff out the thing you're afraid of. True as breath, they wanted to snuff her out. Not just the people, but the guards and soldiers and politicians.

Dhorena had nothing to fear from one foe.

She wouldn't have even scoffed about facing two.

Four might have caused her to sniffle some, but she'd manage.

Eight would be a headache, and bring a long aching if she survived.

But she knew there were at least a thousand guards or soldiers or sheriffs in Illmiv. If the city wanted to kill her sore enough, they'd kill her, sure enough.

So it was with a sudden soberness she said. "I'm fine. I promise."

The gaze of the judge—of all the judges now—was blazing at her, ready to see her dead.

"Maybe," the woman said. "But it seems to us you might have gone feral. Like your father."

"I haven't."

"Maybe," said the woman again. "Maybe if there was a way you could prove that to us?"

Dhorena knew better than to agree to a task untold, so she just waited silently for the woman to whisper it to her. The woman didn't disappoint in one regard even as she did in another.

"Maybe," said the woman yet again. "If you killed the Wildman you brought back with you?"

"No," Dhorena said, too fast. "I don't want to kill him. I want to turn him loose. The ... the Wilderlands will have their way with him."

The middling judge shook her head. "Afraid that can't happen," she said. "Law states that all outsiders who kill Valforian men must perish. As you told us, he was part of the clan that attacked your caravan on the Road. He must die, and you must kill him, unless you've turned wild yourself."

"I killed Valforian men," Dhorena whispered.

"Men who attacked you," the judge explained, then noted the body of Zacharie still being sopped up nearby. "Or accepted your challenge. These were men who were ready to die, for duty or title. Besides, you are no outsider. You are the daughter of a Mayness and acting Mayness until your mother arrives to resume her seat."

"I see." An easy lie that hurt to speak.

The judges waited. "So ... will you do it?"

Though the crowd around barely even shuffled or stuttered, Dhorena couldn't shake the notion that they were laughing at her. Laughing and laughing and laughing at the spot she'd been fixed in.

Dhorena said, "I'll do it."

"Ah," the judge quickly grunted away the blush of shock. "No surprise there I suppose. Killing the monster who kidnapped you, why wouldn't you? I like it. I will send for him. Yes. I think you will be a good Mayness until your mother returns. Here's hoping you follow more after her than ... well, I've said enough."

The judge bowed and backed away, hurrying to get back to the podium, to gossip more with the other judges.

Zacharie bled nearby, only now were soldiers shuffling to move the body, which proved a mightsome task, heavy as that corpse was with armor and jewels that did his soul no good now. Other soldiers were sent scuttling to get Knalc from his prison.

All this happened as Dhorena just stood, red and sinful before her people.

She had nothing to do but stand before them as they watched her, eyeing the blood of the man she'd swift-slain dripping off her. Until, with heat and air, the blood began to crack and harden over her skin. She felt every drop against her flesh-form.

It's hard to say what Dhorena thought in those minutes that petered away while waiting for those soldiers to bring Knalc to her. Not 'cause I don't know what she was thinking, but because I do.

When they finally brought out Knalc, lifted so his feet dragged against the cobble court, he was planted there for her at the base of the Sword Tower. Tied and bound and helpless.

He looked up at her, and though Dhorena doubted any had told him what was 'bout to happen, she could tell by the resigned look in his eyes he had a hardy-notion.

"A public execution," one of the other judges shouted from the podium. "Of one of those barbarians guilty of crimes against Illmiv and all Valforian cities. Mayness, you may proceed when you are most ready."

Her father's sword, her mother's knife, both were still wet with blood from their latest kill. With all the sense of one of the mist-mad, she stumbled toward him, barely thinking about what she did, but with the awful knowing of what she had to do tickling the corner of her every thought and movement. It wasn't many thoughts or motions afore she was standing over him, sword in hand, and shaking like the tail of a thunder-snake.

He just looked up at her.

"I never asked you," she whispered to him, quiet so that no eager ears could hear, and in Wildertongue so that none would understand. *"What's your name?"*

Some say he lied to her, that he gave her false name. Others say he didn't speak words at all, that he kept his mouth shut up 'til the second Death took him. One telling says it like he revealed he was her very father—and that is the most stomach-turning telling I've ever heard of any tale, sure as sin.

I can't say right whether or not it was a lie and I don't know a soul who could fully know lie from truth for certain-straight, even from a soul you know bosom-close. But I know the name he told her, since it's the name I call him in this telling. Since it's the name I heard as I strained my ears to hear-clear.

"Knalc," is what he whispered back.

She'd heard him true, but she wanted to be sure, so that if they met in another life she might know him. For Valforians know that all you keep in any life after this one is your name and the names of those you knew and liked in life. Those names stay with you whether you're flung high or fall low. They are etched on your soul like cracks in clay. *"Say it again."*

"Knalc."

She nodded and stood up straight. Stance wide, now.

It'd be a lie to tell you she didn't want to kill him. Here was the man who'd murdered-cold her mother, her milk-giver. It'd likewise be a lie to tell you she lusted for his death. She couldn't know all of what he'd done or why he'd done it in the bramble-twisted roads of living, but she understood enough.

Her sword was heavy, but still she adorned it with vengeance—she lifted it.

Her hands were shaking, but still she marked their aim—she tightened them.

Her eyes were wet but still they held fire—she focused them.

Never blinking, never wavering, but made stiff with the weight of what she had to do, she brought her blade to blow, and blow and blade bought bitter blood.

This ends as all stories must.

In silence.

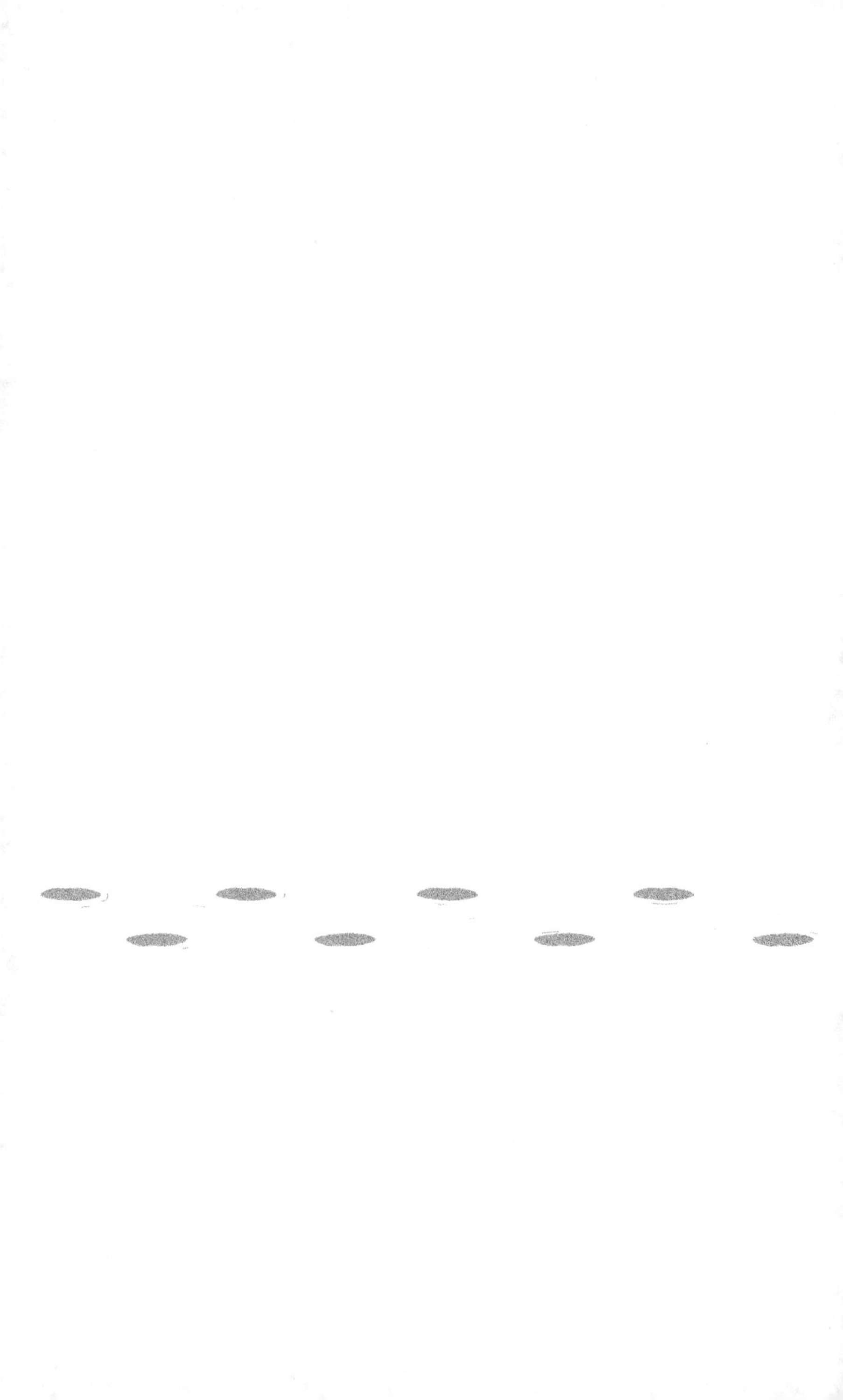

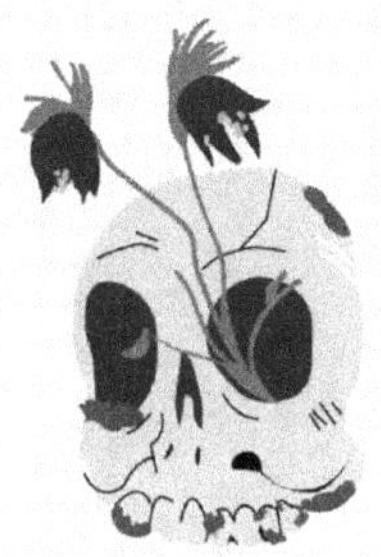

A
THIRD
NIGHT

YOU SHOULD NOT HAVE COME looking for me, child.

The wind is strong, Pappa Sun has not shown his face for days on days on days, and I have survived more winters than you can count. I led you through most of yours. The winter will not take me. No, no, no, there are greater things that have a claim to my life—wilting though it is.

You heard of what them hunters who came back saw in their venturing. A long and twisting beast that looked more fit for deep and dusty waters than winter forest, with teeth too tenfold to count.

If you've marked my stories well, then you'll know that those words near perfectly describe the Great Stone-Licker.

There's a creature that ought not be in the wild wood of our world. He ought to be fish-feasting in deep and distant waters that run colder than even winter air. But I have a notion why he's here.

It's a story I never told you, I won't try to word weave you with the long, but I'll arm you with the short: many many years ago, when I ferried you across white waters on our journey to where we are now, I dealt with that bottom feeder for fair passage—it's a deal I made with no intention to keep. I ferried you through and thought for many years that if I kept to dry stone and dirt, that deal would die.

But that evil eel has clear crawled out of his wave-bed to collect. I suppose I'll have to meet him soon enough and do what can be done to be rid of him. It's not a thing for you to mind.

I know, I know, it's a story I never told you. But you could fill a grave or two with all the tales I never told.

I won't tell you more about ol' Stone-Licker, but I reckon I should finish the tale I been telling these past few days. Or, more like, start the story that comes after.

I ain't never told this part before and am like never to tell it again.

Ay, get as comfortable as you can in this wild and weary place. Give me just a moment or two to remember.

… Yes … Yes.

I have it now.

This is a story you ought to know and it's best you know it from me.

It's about you.

I

THERE WAS A GIRL ONCE.

A long, winding way back, there was a girl who lived in a mightsome tower so tall and regal that all gods and ghouls feared it.

In that tower, this girl lived alone, ate alone, and filled her walls with a tally of her empty days. Yes, she was alone even though she ruled that tower and all who lived under it. The closest thing to company she kept were the meetings she'd be called to where she'd sit and listen to people talk and sign what they asked her to sign and tell little lies.

"My mother is Mayness," she would tell the judges, "and she is coming home and I will rule in her place until she does."

She'd leave and go to her quarters where the company she kept became messages and missives from those who didn't care if she lived or died, and who—like as not—would have preferred the latter. She'd sit and scribble responses peppered with more of her fibbings.

"Thank you for conducting trade with us in the city of Illmiv," she might write. "We here value the partnership between our two cities and are pleased that the shared vigilance of our soldiers has repulsed all attacks on our caravans that come from the monstrous Wildmen."

She was Mayness of that glorious and shining city; the best city in the best civilization that mortal sweat had yet wrought. She was happy. Another little lie.

We all tell ourselves such things, child, and over time, this girl's little lies stacked up as tower-tall as the room she lived in. These lies were easy to live with. To tell it true—it was because of these lies she still lived.

It also made it easy for most of the judges and captains and couriers.

"Why worry about some sapling woman sitting in her mother's chair?" They'd say behind doors they thought she couldn't hear through. "Soon enough, her mother will be back. Or else, the girl will learn to keep the continuity her mother provided. In all cases commerce continues as ever."

And though their whispers made her stomach boil, the girl knew better than to rope up the Road workings out of rage and simple spite. She didn't bother them none and they didn't prod her past their piddling papers. So she sat and signed and stayed quiet when she could.

Yet, once a week—at the most lonesome hour of the night— the girl turned into a monster.

She'd wake in sweat drenched desire and she'd hear—pouring over the stone walls, welling up from the cobble of streets below— the song of the Wilderlands. Though she might try to bed bury herself, the hammering of that tune wouldn't let her rest. So she'd shimmy and sly-sneak from her tower, hobbling 'cross stone and shingle, 'cross roof and rafter, all to quell her hearing and hide out in the Wilderlands.

She'd make her way to the speck of a hole she'd long since chipped from the wall for wizard promises. She'd belly crawl her way beyond the wall and wed herself to the Wilder-song that strung her hence.

In her running from the wall, she'd look at Mamma Moon and pray the goddess would not let her hobble home when Pappa Sun came 'round in the sky. After her prayer, she would sink away from the moon and stars and into bush and branch and root and soil and dirt and death and the bosom-blossom of Grandma Dirt.

She knew she was a monster because her father had heard and heeded the same fever song and been painted red for running off to it. She knew she was a monster because she'd once painted a man red—a man she liked well as one can like a murderer—for having been born in, and fate-twisted by, the Wilderlands.

And she knew she was a monster because she couldn't even stand to stay monstrous, for no matter how hard she prayed, when she saw the signs of Pappa Sun painting the sky, she'd creep shy-shamed back to her tower.

When she was wrapped in bed and blanket and little lies, she'd say that never again would she let the Wilderlands wile her back. Then, when it inevitably did, she would lay on the bosom-blossom of Grandma Dirt and tell her that she would not let the sun scare her back home. But it always did, because she could not stomach her sins in the garish daylight. She knew it was wrong to run away and, when she did, her shame yanked her home until her feet paddled her back to what she'd been yanked from.

This went on for years, or days, or decades, and the girl found herself sometimes staying out for longer, but always shame scruff-scorned her home with the coming of Pappa Sun.

It might have stayed like that, I think. With the girl, Dhorena— by now a woman—living 'hind those hallowed walls, feeling hollowed out inside 'cept for when she wandered Wilder-ward and could breath for just a bit until the dawn burned her face with the shadow of shame.

Maybe it all could have hummed on like that. Maybe she could have lived her days in that tower and turned wild weekly 'til the day she died, letting herself—once ripe with wrinkles like I am now—lay in Grandma Dirt and dream of her mother and brother and father until she turned to naught but a freckle on Grandma Dirt's face.

There's a beauty of sorry sort to that I think, but it wasn't to be.

She thought herself shrew-sneaky and fox-clever, and she was. Yet in all her goings and returnings, she'd been malice-marked by one whose eyes burned with the light of Brother Hatred.

THERE WAS A GIRL ONCE.

A long, winding way back, there was a girl who had learned wrath at the age where the hate you've been saddled with don't shake off. They say she'd seen her parent killed by some feral faced brute of the Wilderlands.

She had no love for the Wilderlands or the woman living lofty in the Sword Tower.

This girl had seen Dhorena, fresh from killing her father, ascend to Illmiv's most illustrious station. She had watched as that woman, still painted with the blood of her blood, profaned that high seat with her presence. So, soul-wreathed with vengeance, this girl set her sights on climbing within a knife's tickle of Dhorena.

In the course of years, that girl became one of the judges who Dhorena would sit among and pass papers with.

The judge knew the way the world ought to be. She knew that walls were built on two sides: one side to keep the Wilderlands out and one to keep Valforians in. The judge knew that every time the woman, her Mayness, warped Wilder-ward, some Valforian was lost to the Wilderlands and some Wilderlands found its way back into Illmiv when the Mayness returned. Dhorena was breaking the boundary both ways, and the judge—oh, child—she could not let that stand.

It was because of this judge that Dhorena encountered a paper she couldn't sign in silence as she had so many. When the paper was passed around, every ass at that great stone table inked their inclination for its quill-furnishings. It was only as it came to the Mayness that someone minded those scribblings.

It was seeing the word "Wilderlands" scribbled so weedishly through the document that made her halt her quill-quelling. She picked up the paper and scowled through it, face-to-feet, while the eyes of every judge and sheriff there scrutinized her.

"What is this?" Dhorena asked, horror-slapped by the hubris.

"A brilliant bit of legislation, if you ask me," grumbled one grandfatherly judge.

"'Legislation'?" Dhorena reeled. "This is a war declaration."

Dhorena had never thought herself humorsome, but she got that council chortling. Save for one; the judge who'd whipped up the bill bent her lips in a snowy smile toward Dhorena and let nothing else loose.

When at last the laughter lagged, a captain wiped a tear from his cheek. "A war declaration? War with who, Mayness? The rocks and stones? The trees and birds?"

Had she spoken as her tongue bid, she would have lashed back: "Yes, the rocks and stones and birds and trees. And the gods and monsters and men that wait for us outside those walls! You and so many have it so good in this horrible city, why would you risk that?"

But shame and preservation leashed her loquaciousness and she thought of some more apple-ripe remarks.

"This proposition," she said, "if I read it right, would double the size of the land we keep behind our wall over the course of decades. These walls have stood as they are since the founders, in their wisdom, put them up. For centuries that has been enough to hold back the Wilderlands. Why risk that?"

"For the sake of our people, who we are charged with protecting," the girl, the judge who penned the paper, spoke with a voice like summer's dying. "Over centuries we have become crowded behind these wisdom wrought walls. With space at a premium, we have relied on trade for food rather than homegrown goods. That trade is often stalled when snow comes, or raided when the Wilderfolk wish it. Expanding the wall, incentivizing crop growth, creating work with the need for laborers on the wall, beating back the ever creeping Wilderlands—I see little to risk and much to gain."

Nods and affirmations filled the air, with only Dhorena stone-staring back at this judge who met her unblinking bane in kind.

As the council settled and looked back to their Mayness, she still stared at this irksome girl. "I will not sign it."

The girl leaned back, for she did not have to speak as every voice at that table chimed off her words for her:

"Now, Mayness, be reasonable."

"This is a proposition long overdue!"

"The council—representatives from across districts—all agree."

"Not approving this proposal would be a gross neglect of your office."

"Our unanimous decision compels you to do the same!"

The hair on the back of Dhorena's neck stood the way it often would when she was in the Wilderlands and the howl of coywolves would draw nearer and nearer. She almost reached for her steel, but knew this wasn't the sort of pack she could slay—'sides, she hadn't brought her blade to a meeting such as this.

So she stood and slammed her hands on the table, silencing the council's chittering.

Slowly, like a snake swallowing some corpulent carcass, she looked each leader there in the eye. 'Til she came to the judge who'd brought this bill to her. The judge just smiled back.

Dhorena took the papers, flipped through them again, sorted and straightened them, and filed them into the roaring fireplace that lit the chamber.

Gasps filled the room as the white pages turned black and withered and fluttered through the chamber as ash and soot.

"I," Dhorena said, "will not approve such a proposal. This will not be mentioned to me again. I am Mayness of Illmiv and I have spoken."

She heel-spun toward the door and was most of the way marched out when the judge finally spoke again.

"Thank you for your wisdom, Mayness," she said. "I suppose it is important we have the perspective of one who, on many occasions, turns mad and drooling and dances, lustily and unsanctioned, into the Wilderlands."

Dhorena stopped. She looked over her shoulder and spoke before the cold sweat she felt coming could stain her clothes. "You speak out of turn."

The council was already muttering.

The judge morphed her face in fox-mock surprise. "Do I? Then I apologize most profusely. I was out of line. Thank you for correcting me, Mayness."

The muttering was growing and all Dhorena could hear was howling.

She straightened up, stepped out of the room, and—once the door was closed—she ran.

Like a hunted beast, through winding halls and twisting stairs, she retreated to her empty room at the top of her shining tower and she locked the door and she waited for them to come for her, making herself comfortable near the entrance with the weapons of her forbearers.

She waited.

And she waited.

And more she waited.

Days passed without so much as the flutter of fingers at her door.

Wake-crazed and weary, she eventually let herself slouch toward her bed. When she woke, she was surprised not to find herself sleep slaughtered, nay, instead, she found mundane messages delivered through her door.

So, she went back to the lonely rhythm she knew from before her fright. Somehow, though, she fought the song of the Wilderlands.

Dhorena did avoid the judges and sheriffs and captains where she could in her days and it was only when she was duty wrangled back to one of the meetings that she sat among them again. When she did, there was no mention of the proposal they'd tried to push on her. No mention of pulling apart a portion of the wall to build it up stronger and wider than ever before, to swallow up a swath of Green with the cobblings of mortals.

But there was still the girl, the judge who'd penned the proposal, sitting and smiling—though small-like—all through each tedious meeting.

Soon the slow return to rhythm became a time-telling tempo yet again. Dhorena was shocked that she never caught musk or mutter of the bill, her outburst, or anything of the like.

Nearly a year passed—maybe more would have hummed by in that weathered tempo, but Dhorena finally felt it again. Like a warbler is called with its season, like bees fly fixed, she heard the buzz-hum of the Wilderlands again. She had staved it off long and the song's reprise, after all her fighting, found her flimsy. The Mayness scarce realized she was following the call until she was squirrel-scurrying down the side of her tower and leaping like a cottontail from roof to roof.

Child, she might have made the trip with her eyes closed,

guided only by the scent of wild wind. Roof and rafter, rock and road she crossed, hungry to breathe in the gods and the growing world you've come to know.

She did not make it to the Wilderlands that night.

Nay. As she rambled 'long her usual route, she was stopped by sheer sight.

That mighty wall that had played tyrant to her all her living days was pulled apart here and there. Not sundered in full, only in part so it might be stacked more sinister. For every stone missing in that gap there was a guards, for every deficit square foot of defense were three workers. Even at this hour of the night, the scent of burning oil lamps and the ping of pick axes sang a song of industry, expansion, and thunderous treachery. A plan she'd been privy to pulled all these things in didactic discord.

She heard the howl of coywolves and, fear-fraught, she slinked back to her quiet tower where she spent the night grinding her teeth, choking on wrath and terror.

In the morning, as the sun set the sky blushing, she called an emergency meeting of her council.

"You all have deliberately disobeyed me!" she spat at them. "I walked about last night to find a wall torn apart by the ambition of plotting fools who have deluded themselves with the farce that the bill I burned so long ago was of any worth. You conducted your business as though I would not notice and now you have been discovered." She looked at the cold and smiling judge. "Do you, do any of you, have anything to say for yourselves?"

For a time, if you really strained your ears and knew what to listen for, I bet you could have heard the song of those pick axes echoing in the crannies of that chamber. Until—

"... You did not walk about last night," said one captain, older than some. "Not like civilized folk do, anyhow. If you had, your guards would have noted it to me."

Shame and anger boiled her face. "And now you admit to spying on me! I'll see you hanged! Would any other collaborators like to come forward? Do so now and the repercussions may merely be imprisonment beneath the Sword Tower for the rest of your natural days. Speak now!"

No one spoke. Until—

"You actually didn't notice," one of the jitterier judges offered. "For, well, for quite a time. Anyone walking the city, or—by the gods—who bothered to speak with citizens, could have told you what was happening."

Her left fist racked the table while her right hand pointed at the aghast judge. "Hanged! Would anyone else like to speak against your Mayness?"

An old judge, old enough now to be ancient—the same who had incited the duel between Dhorena and Zacharie—stood.

"You are not Mayness."

Dhorena hissed like steel. "I beg your pardon?"

"As you should," the ancient judge said. "It's your mother who was Mayness. You had said she yet lived in the Wilderlands. Yet that was years back, she is, by now, long dead. You are not Mayness of Illmiv or anywhere else."

It's wondersome how much of a fight a soul might put up even when doom has drawn upon them like a fit cloak.

"Hanged!" Dhorena screamed. "Guards! Guards! I have men with necks that need tightened, to keep the owners from vomiting up more madness. Guards!"

Wondersome.

"Guards?"

The guards remained cozy by the door and the whole of the council stood, 'cept for the judge who just sat and smiled.

One of the captains stepped toward Dhorena. "Now all that

you said to us, wasn't very nice, eh? I think you should apologize."

She spat in his face, buried her elbow in his gut, hammered him to the floor, and would have done more if the guards didn't get to her just then. They found that seizing her was like trying to wrangle a mad thunder-snake in its death throes—but she had no bite, no steel, and so they managed.

The pride-pricked captain heaved himself to his feet and staggered to stand over her. He spat a glob of blood on her face. A scattered laugh went through the council chambers; they'd found a goddess they could kill for not going to their liking.

She Wilder-hissed at them all. "*Horse fuckers!*"

"Guards," he slurred past a swelling lip. "This chamber is for council members only. Take this interloper to her cage while we consider what to do with a mongrel such as her. If she's seen outside of her quarters, kill her as though she were a foam-mad mutt."

She roared and, like a wild beast, they pulled her from that chamber. Two guards became four, and four turned to eight, and they dragged her to her room. They threw her to the floor and slammed the door behind them.

They didn't bother to take the weapons she kept in her room; she could not fight the city. They didn't bother to lock her door, for where could she go? She looked through rage soaked eyes at the city below, Illmiv bubbled to its brim with hate for her.

Like a caged laughing-cat, she paced her room.

"Maybe," she muttered to herself. "I fight off who I can. I am still fast and nimble—I can run when I need. I could make it to the Wilderlands. I could make for one of the other cities, or, better yet, make it on my own in the greener places of the world."

But they were empty plans.

She knew she could not make it to another Valforian city. And if she fled to the Wilderlands, so what? She'd be alone in the naked world with no kin to kindle fire with. Just a sadness of a different sort than her tower room.

Eventually, she stopped pacing and just sat and slept and dreamed that, rather than kill her, they might rend her nameless and give her a red coat and a duty. That flavor of tragedy, at least, might keep her going while letting her taste the Wilderlands again—though she would have no one to play ward to as she had not a single friend or lover or child who she had betrayed. Only the vast throngs of strangers she lived above.

It was night when her door opened and the smiling judge entered her room. The girl was spotless from crown to sole. Hair tied in a perfect bun, spectacles exactly in fashion, and robes without blemish or crease.

"Hello, Dhorena," the young judge smiled, locking the door behind her.

A spark of hate flickered in Dhorena's gut, but it was quick quenched by the sorrow-mire she'd been soaking in.

"Hello," Dhorena answered.

The judge made herself cozy in a plush chair Dhorena realized she herself had barely ever sat in.

The judge cleared her throat. "I hope you've been comfortable."

"You don't."

"Oh, I do. I do. Because I think you deserve the guilt of comfort before your trial and execution."

"What do I have to feel guilty for? You're the one who's led a coup against me."

"Well, in point of fact, you would need to actually be a ruler for it to be a coup. I say this is more of a … correction."

Dhorena squinted at the girl, hoping she might somehow see something about her she couldn't so far spot. "Why?"

"If there is an error there ought to be a correction."

"There are many errors. Why me?"

The judge smiled, teeth like gravestones. "You are the biggest error of them all."

"I wasn't bothering anyone."

The judge stood and walked around the room. After a few flaps of time, her eyes settled on the sword Dhorena had on her wall. With steady hands, the judge pulled the Valforian steel from the wall and let her fingers lick its length.

"You don't remember me."

Dhorena couldn't tell for certain if she was speaking to her or the sword.

"We met," the judge went on. "Years before I was a judge." She looked over her shoulder at Dhorena.

Dhorena held her gaze, still searching for something she couldn't see.

The judge went on. "When you first came back, when we all believed your mother might really be in the Wilderlands. Somehow nearly no one but me saw you the way you always were."

Dhorena stayed silent.

"Am I not worth speaking to?" The judge clutched the sword, her hand shuttersome on the hilt.

"It seems to me you have a mind to say what you'll say, whether I whisper back or not."

The judge smiled. Cold, hard, patient. She rooted herself in standing there, eyeing Dhorena up and down. "When you came back to Illmiv, thirteen men died because of your returning."

"Fourteen."

"Thirteen noble men of Illmiv, my father among them."

Dhorena tried not to show the shame that twisted within her.

She stagger-stuttered and groped through her memory to see

if she could count the men she'd killed in her first days and match a face to the judge before her. It could have been any of the men she and Knalc had cut-killed on the road outside the city. It could have been Zacharie himself.

The smile slipped away, but the judge was cold and patient as ever. "Do you remember who my father was?"

Dhorena thought to fib, to guess that Zacharie had been her father. But the bends of the young judge's cheeks and chompers, the shadow of her brow, none of it didn't seemed quite right to be of Zacharie's ilk. So she told her true.

"I have no idea."

Cold and patient.

"I suppose you wouldn't," the judge said. "You have shared a council with me these many months and I suspect you don't know my name. Why should you know his face?"

"I'm sorry."

"You're not."

"I am," Dhorena said. "I don't feel bad for you, but I'm sorry that happened to you."

"No … not yet you're not." She stepped toward Dhorena. "Perhaps you will be sorry when the city sees to your sins and deems death the best end to you. Right before we burn through the Wilderlands you so love to gallivant through."

"… was your father Zacharie?"

"That question offends me."

"Zacharie took everything from my father, all but killing him. That's why I killed Zacharie. He pushed my mother from her royal seat, leaving her to die in the Wilderlands, that's why I killed Zacharie. He, the Vox, everyone in this city told me my brother had no soul and so, when my brother died, I couldn't mourn him. That's why I killed Zacharie.

"When I got home, I couldn't accept all the blood and lost loved ones had been for nothing. I knew neither me nor … the Wildman would be able to make it back to the Wilderlands. I knew he'd done what he needed to do by coming here. His coming here was done in part to protect me, which is why I killed him."

The judge tilted her head. "You mean Knalc?"

A chill chattered its way up Dhorena's spine, spurring her to stand. She hadn't heard that name mouthed off since she'd killed the man who bore it.

"How do you know that name?"

"I was there when you killed him," the judge said. "Maybe not everyone in the crowd heard your Wilder-whispering, but I understood enough of who you were then to know you asked his name before you killed him. A courtesy you did not extended to my father!"

"Only I heard that name. How do you know that name?"

The judge approached her, sword still in hand, until they were within steel-strike of one another.

"I told you, I heard the name. Just because when you were my age you were dull and stubborn doesn't mean I am."

Dhorena glanced at her father's steel still in the young judge's hand. "Why are you here?"

The cold and patient curve of her lips frosted the judge's face again.

"I just wanted you to know before you die, that what is happening is law, yes. But, it is also just, and it is personal. I wanted you to know that you are lower than the lowest stone on the wall. I wanted you to know that you are a monster."

Child, the lowest stone on the wall knows where it sits, and most monsters know their teeth well enough to reckon themselves as such. But the judge was not done, seeing that Dhorena was not word-wounded, she dug deeper.

"A shame you took after your father and will have your name struck from the Mural of Maynes as well. You will die and no one will care, just as when he died. Were it not justice, it would be sad that a nameless man was even more unmade so that his daughter could undo herself."

Dhorena quick snuffed the spark that sputtered in her stomach. She stood still.

The young judge went on.

"A better death than your mother, who maybe was trying her best, only to become the whore of the beast you killed upon your return to the city. I hear the Wilderfolk often slay each other during copulation, it's supposed to make the pleasure greater for the survivor. What a joy killing your mother must have been for Knalc and killing Knalc must have been for you."

Dhorena breathed deep to snuff again her stomach-spark.

"I wish your brother had had a soul so that he at least could have been raised out of the filth he came from when he died. Did you kill him too? Did you get joy from wiping that nameless thing from the face of this earth? Daughters disappoint their parents frequently, so it is not unique that you have failed there. But your negligence as a sibling is unique—how shameful that you either killed him yourself, or that you failed to protect your tongue-dumb, idjit of a brother!"

Dhorena caught the motion of the Valforian steel mid-breath but was too late—

Blood stained the girl's flesh.

The young judge stopped as sanguine spittle bubbled to her lips, her cold eyes melting. Melting …

Dhorena had been too late to stop herself.

She'd put her father's blade between her adversary's ribs easy as sin; simple as breath.

"I'm sorry," Dhorena said, and was horror-struck to find she didn't mean it.

The judge slowly sank to the floor, coughing and cloying for speech, but achieving only loss of blood and breath. Snarling, she spat red in Dhorena's face.

"Please! I'm sorry!" Dhorena screamed, trying desperately to mean it, trying desperately to feel some soul-splintering or sin-shook notion of what she'd done.

The young judge wailed soundlessly on the floor, groaning, which made little more than a seedling sound. Her eyes were hateful and longing.

Tears slipped from Dhorena's eyes at the sorrow she didn't feel as she cradled the judge—the girl—there in her room, in her lair. "I'm sorry." She thought if she said it enough times she might make it true. "I'm sorry … I'm sorry. I'm sorry! I'm sorry!"

That's how Dhorena knew she was a monster; in her sorry-sorrow, she found she'd failed to notice that the soul had slipped from the shell a long while ago.

Dhorena wailed and waited.

For some reason, the gods—cackling and calloused though they've always been—pitied the woman. It was a long while, long past the hour where someone should have come looking, that anyone came for Dhorena.

She was red as sin when they did. She'd never stopped cradling the body of the judge, who kept staring at the ceiling, colder and more patient than ever. Waiting for her killer to be discovered and for hasty justice to be dealt.

The sun had sunk from sight again when she finally heard the rattling of her door.

"*I'm sorry,*" she whispered, but it didn't matter how or what she whispered. Those cold eyes never answered back.

Child, you mind now that the judge's body was cold and growing colder all through the unwinding of what comes next.

"Mayness!" a voice called from outside her room, rapping and rattling her door. "We need you!"

"It's time for my trial," the woman said. "I'm ready."

The racking and ruckus at her door grew.

"No, Mayness! We're under attack!"

"I'm guilty," the woman said. "I just … I want you to know that now. I'm guilty."

"Mayness—"

"You ought to have that judge girl kill me. She ought to lop away my head and bleed me on the cobblestones."

"We need you! Mayness—"

"I killed her father too and I don't even remember which dead man he was. But we were all fine with it. All the city let me kill men, like the Wilderfolk let Knalc kill my mother. People don't care whether you kill behind walls or out in the Wilderlands. All they care is who you are while you do the killing and how you do it."

The ruckus at her door had stopped. The voice had faded.

"I think I deserve to die. Isn't that horrible? I think I deserve to die and here I am with the gall to keep living. I don't think I can unlock the door for you though. I … I think I deserve to die, I can't bring myself to unlock the door, but I can't bring myself to leave the city. Isn't that horrible?"

The room, cold and damp and dreary, was suddenly lit. Bright and red and roaring.

From outside the window came a wicked fire-flash and the screaming of unyielding stone diminished. Rock turned to dust as Grandma Dirt cried out.

It was fire indeed that did it, but fiercer fire than the one that started my last story.

This was fire made by Wastefolk. Fire that snaked up the wall along the cracks of construction—living, burning ropes that bled into those walls—indomitable—pulling them asunder. Time flew overhead and let out a warble, for if those walls ever fell—and they did—Time would witness it. Time witnesses the death of all things and will be there to watch Death wither for want of souls to scavenge.

But those walls came down, and as they did, Dhorena rose red from her floor and went to her balcony. As she looked out at a world drowning in red, her first thought was that Death himself had come for her.

III

THERE WAS A CHILD ONCE.

A child who did not deserve all the briary the world had waiting for them.

But look at me, tripping ahead of myself like some green and over eager teller. The child will come, but first, the blast that burned away the wall.

That blast sent dust and ash and screaming every which way and let a legion of Wastefolk scurry into the city like a murder of painted shadows. Oils and elixirs, brews milked from hell-hives, were thrown and tossed onto house and stone and screaming city-folk.

So mightsome was their attack that, when Dhorena waded out onto her balcony, not only were rock and stone wreathed in flames, but the stars themselves were bloodied in the heavens.

Long it was she watched.

Watched the home she'd fought so hard to come back to burn. Like a caravan on the Road.

"I'm sorry," she whispered to her ash choked home.

Even as she watched the burning, her mind went back to the Wilderlands, just beyond the crumbling walls.

Never mind how long she stood there, watching the smashing

and soiling of stone and souls. Long enough for more than one stone to break, long enough for Death to unstitch more souls in a single swoop than he had in eons. The woman began to realize she was waiting.

At first, she thought it was Death she was counting toward. That made her smile. She was ready. Ready to let all her lies and sin come blazing back to her. She closed her eyes ready to surrender to Death, as all must eventually, yet before her lids could stick shut, she caught a light.

Not the light of the hateful, rapacious fire roaring through Illmiv.

The light she saw was distant and white and silent. A silent, pure white lightning against a cloudless sky.

You ever see such a thing? No, no one has.

"Did you see that?" the Mayness of the burning city called to the room behind her, cold and patient. *"Did you see that?"*

There's a story I've found in my world-wandering, one of the few I reckon is the same atween all folk: Waste, Wall, and Wilder.

Whether you worship the Vulture's Eye, Aprheus, or Mamma Moon and Pappa Sun—human life, they say, comes from the heavens. I'll tell you the wilder-how of it as that's the way it happened and it was in witnessing that happening that heathen gods were finally unfastened from that girl.

Back when Sun and Moon were making Green and smiling rainbows, they too made mortal man to walk the earth and celebrate their union. They shaped life from the flesh of Grandma Dirt using a single brilliant flash—the color of Moon but heaven-hot as Sun's smile. Like lightning, the beam fell from the heavens.

This is what I realized in seeing that beam. While Sun and Moon are sunder-spun more oft than not, they each hold a bit of their meeting-might inside of them. That power gets flung about when they can't stomach the horrors humans wring from one another.

I didn't full know that when I saw it then, but I knew it was a mightsome thing to witness. A miracle cutting through the pure black of night.

I stood, I watched, and Death did not take me.

"Did you see that?"

And like a humming-hawk spurred by Winterwind, I knew in my bones the haven I had to head toward.

"I'm sorry," I whispered to the room, to the city I had fought back to all that time ago. I tell you, I wanted to save that city. I really did. Affixed by hate or hankering, the place you're birthed stays in the meat of your heart; I'd seen that which I hated and hankered for go red and burn before. It's enough to make you love a thing again, even if it's only ash and mean memory.

You cannot save burning things, child, not when they're as flame-swallowed as Illmiv was. That's an ending you can't interrupt. But to tell you true, I was Mayness, I couldn't ignore the screams of cooking souls in full. I still hear them sometimes while I sleep ...

Yet I did what I could then-there. I seized a coat the color of my father before his sin. I took the knife my mother wielded before her demise. I prayed to the soul of my brother. I looked back one more time at the room—a cold patient place 'bout to be bubbling with fire.

And I left.

Child, I am a teller of worthy stature, but I can't weave together the words to tell you how paint-perfect—how *pain-perfect*—it feels to leave a rotting thing to rot.

I took to the roofs and rafters as smoke and screams and souls rose around me. Even through my boots, I could feel the burning of the city below me. I never looked down though, save to make sure when I jumped from one spot to another that I was not leaping straight to my own demise.

Sometimes I lost my footing, sometimes I caught a terrible smog in my lungs, but nothing that brought Death to me.

Death was occupied.

I whispered a wizard-cant taught to me long ago, and the Wastefolk slithering over stones and through the streets didn't mind or mark me none.

Over spell-wrought rubble, down blast-made ruins and into the Wilderlands, I ran, raging toward the place I'd seen that lightning-like strike. Happenstance would have it that much of the death and burning the Wastefolk had wrought through the Wilderlands cut a clean trail.

There were no silver tips or laughing-cats to fight. I didn't need to kill any wizards or best any gods or ghouls.

I didn't need to give an arm or swallow my honor to get to you. The way was easy.

There, somewhere along that clean-cut trail, I found the spot—a heaven hewn crater—where I saw that beam fall. At the center of that spot, was you.

You were a suckling child in the make of Mamma Moon, laying newborn in the Wilderlands, in the wake of the Wastefolk, and in the arms of a Valforian once I plucked you up. You looked up at me with waiting eyes I couldn't stomach to hate. Shaking like a winter-leaf, under the gaze of Mount Hush-bee, I found you.

Somehow, when I picked you up, I judged your weight right. Lifting you up wasn't too easy or too hard. And you looked at me, pudgy and silent for a baby, and I worried for a breath that you were mute-made. Then I realized I didn't care.

If you were mute-made, it would be hard for you to draw out coywolves or laughing-cats or silver tips.

I don't know the will of the gods, child. With little exception, they are hateful, they are horrid, and they smite and spit at humans for simple sport. But you, I think, were one of their rare blessings. I say, your soul—twisted by the horrors and hardship of the world—was given a second chance 'cause Mamma Moon or Grandma Dirt saw that you could get to better living with a soul like yours.

I say, my soul—warped by the hate and heartlessness of the world—got a second shot at loving something for the right reasons.

I don't know the will of the gods, child, but the warmth of gods' breath was still on you.

Valforians know that all you keep in any life after this one is your name and the names you knew and liked in life. They stay with you whether you're flung high or fall low. They're etched on your soul like cracks in clay.

"That's who you are, isn't it?" I whispered to you in the tongue I had not savored for far too long.

Tears slicked up my cheeks before splashing down onto yours.

And, toothless, you bit me—hard. But you did not draw blood and that is how I knew for certain who I held.

I smiled wide and white as winter-root. I'd finally found you.

"I'm sorry," I said, and was warmed to find I meant it.

Acknowledgements

I imagine it's possible to write a book in less than ten years. I've yet to confirm that, but I imagine it's possible.

Thankfully, creating *The Wilderlands* was a less involved decade than some of my other projects. I wrote a version of the opening chapter in 2013—after reading *Moby Dick*—before quickly realizing I did not have the skills I needed to do this particular story justice. It wasn't until about five years later—after an English degree that introduced me to *Beowulf,* and independently reading *Something Wicked This Way Comes*—that I felt like I might be able to string together something close to what I'd imagined.

Therefore thanks, first and foremost, go to my grandmother who gifted me that copy of *Something Wicked.*

I also want to thank Eli for reading a good chunk of this book back in 2018 and then reading it again in 2023 and providing maybe the single best idea for revision I received. I want to equally thank Hannah (for being an ardent fan) as well as Casey (who somehow read this book in just a day) and Kaity (who claims the second and third best ideas I received for final revision).

Thanks as well to Zephin for reading a rather rough early version. I should also thank my mother for her attempts to read even earlier versions and supporting me (though I have a powerful sense that this, perhaps, will not be her favorite book of mine.)

I also want to show appreciation to Marianne, Oscar, Billie, Virginia, Fred, and Jan for reading the first chapter of this, despite it being well outside of their typical genre, and giving earnest feedback.

A massive thanks to Rae for voicing the audiobook and being very patient as I went through that process for the first time.

Thanks as well to Alyssa and Leon for their artistic enthusiasm and Drake, for his general enthusiasm. Much appreciation to the booksellers at Beaverdale Books for brightening my day without fail every time I encounter them.

High thanks go to the cover artist, Sabrina, who powered through the project during a particularly rough set of months. Wendy as well for making sure the inside and outside of this book looks beautiful across formats. Aimée for providing solid feedback and edits during a time where I was terrified of handing this book over to a complete stranger. And Kelsey, for stellar work making an unplanned final pass for edits as the publication date loomed.

Thank you as well, reader, for finding your way here.

R.E. BELLESMITH is the author of "The Wilderlands," his stand-alone adult fantasy novel, and "Light Keeper Chronicle: The Unspoken Prophecy," the first entry in his YA/Middle-grade Fantasy series. Born in Michigan, he now lives in Iowa where he's probably writing (or sleeping) at this very moment. He has never known the song of tricksy Valforian steel or been called to Wilder-wandering. Find more from him at rebellesmith.com.